Clean Western Romance

Counting on the Cowboy

DAISY LANDISH

BEACHES AND TRAILS
PUBLISHING

About the Author

Daisy Landish is a romance and cozy mystery author living in the UK, whose clean and sweet stories have tugged at readers' heartstrings across the pond and beyond. When she's not writing, Daisy spends her time reading, hiking at dawn, and riding into the sunset on her horse, Rosebud.

Join Daisy's Newsletter for updates and giveaways!
www.daisylandishromance.com

facebook.com/daisylandishromance

x.com/daisy_landish

instagram.com/beachesandtrailspublishing

amazon.com/author/daisylandish

bookbub.com/authors/daisy-landish

goodreads.com/Daisy_Landish

Also by Daisy Landish

Prologue

PIPER FUMED. The clock on the television read eleven-thirty pm. She turned it off and took the empty wine bottle and glass to the kitchen. For the third night in a row, her husband had not come home after work. No call, no text.

The previous two nights, he'd given her a load of crap about staying late at work. She knew for a fact that John had left the office today at five. She had watched him drive out of the firm's parking lot with a smile on his face and a spring in his step. She hadn't seen that smile in months.

On both days, he came in just a little before midnight. Piper tightened her robe and rehearsed what she would tell her two-timing husband.

When the car pulled up in the driveway, Piper unlocked the door and stepped out onto the front porch. The headlights from the S.U.V. shone right at her. It had to be plain to see, she was angry. If her crossed arms hadn't given it away, the deep scowl she was aiming at her husband would.

The headlights went off, and the low humming of the car stopped. John climbed out of his car and sighed. The radiant smile of this afternoon had been replaced with the haggard look of someone wanting to avoid confrontation. He picked up his briefcase and started trudging towards the house. John climbed the porch stairs without even sparing a glance at Piper.

Piper was heartbroken. For the better part of the ten years they had been married, they'd greeted each other with kisses and long hugs. Piper tried to keep her anger in check.

"It's almost midnight," she stated.

John stopped with his hand on the doorknob. He didn't turn around or look at her. "Thank you for stating the obvious, Piper."

"I was waiting up for you," Piper answered, turning her head to look at him. The pain in her voice was evident.

"I don't remember asking you to," John answered, before opening the door and stepping into the house.

Piper stood on the porch, trying to breathe. John's reaction had knocked the wind out of her. She couldn't understand how he could be so carefree and cold towards her, even after being married for so long. A lone tear fell down her face, and she wiped it off quickly before following him into the house.

The mood in the living room seemed to have changed since he entered the house. The air was ripe with tension. She had to admit their relationship had disintegrated in the last few months. She had thought they'd just been going through a rough patch. That things would get better.

"How long?" she asked.

John sighed again, his shoulders sagging. He knew enough not to lie.

"A few months," he replied, as he sank into the sofa, his briefcase dropping to the floor beside him.

Piper didn't know what she had done to lose his love, but she was pretty sure that it had something to do with her inability to have children. John loved kids, and he had dreamed of having a large family. For most of their marriage, they had made a conscious effort to conceive. They tried everything possible and finally gave up five years ago. Perhaps he hadn't given up hope.

"Is it serious?" she asked, staring out at the immaculate landscaping of their front lawn.

"She's pregnant," replied John. "I'm so sorry, Piper. I swear I didn't intend for this to happen. I would never want to hurt you..." His voice trailed off.

She had her answer. The fight and anger went out of her. All she felt was numb.

"I need you to leave. Get what you need for a couple of days," said Piper in a mechanical voice.

He got up and came to her, putting an arm around her.

"Don't." She dodged out from under the embrace, not wanting to be touched.

He dropped his arm and headed for the bedroom. Piper continued to stare out the window, without moving.

He came back fifteen minutes later, suitcase in hand. In silence, he retrieved his briefcase with his free hand. When Piper didn't say anything, he opened the door and said, "I'll call you in a few days so we can work things out."

Once he was gone, Piper locked the door and added the chain just in case he decided to come back.

She laid in bed for a long time, staring at the ceiling. Finally, the enormity of what had just happened closed around her. She felt like she would die. The tears came, and she let the sobs wrack her body until she finally fell asleep.

When Piper woke the next morning, the other side of the bed was still empty. It looked just the way it had the night before. With a heavy sigh, she climbed out of bed. The house seemed quieter than normal without him. She made her way to the sitting room, feeling physically and emotionally exhausted.

She made coffee and looked at the list of chores and errands she had planned for the day. There was nothing urgent. An hour later, she hadn't moved from her perch on the stool. She'd been ruminating on last night's revelations. She came to a rather disturbing conclusion. There was nothing she could have done to save her marriage. When the doorbell rang, she jumped. Wearily, she made her way to the door. A glance through the peephole told her it wasn't John. The man looked like a messenger, holding an envelope in his hand.

She unlocked the door but kept the chain in place. "Yes?" she said.

"Are you Piper Hills Baker?" he asked plainly.

"Yes, I'm Piper," she replied, her eyes narrowing.

He thrust the envelope through the opening in the door and said, "You have been served, ma'am." With a nod of the head, he turned and left Piper holding the manila envelope.

"Served?" she wondered out loud as she closed and locked the door.

Then, it dawned on her. Divorce papers. She opened the envelope and took out the forms. They'd been drawn up a few days ago, on the day John had come home late the first time. *Coward,* she thought. He'd probably had the papers in his briefcase all week and was unable to broach the subject with her.

She sighed and considered her options. She could make a fuss and delay the inevitable, but did she even want to at this point? In the end, she decided to take the high road. The settlement was fair, and the faster she signed the papers, the quicker she'd be able to move on with her life.

One

"MOM, I know exactly what I'm doing! I'm not a child anymore," Piper said, her frustration evident in the way she crumpled her napkin and threw it down next to her plate.

"Sweetheart, this is something you have never experienced before! You need to be around family and people that love you right now. I just want to protect you," her mother answered from across the table.

"I understand, mother. But you have to trust me. Going away is best right now. I put everything into my marriage with John, and now I need to find a new purpose for myself," Piper explained.

"You can do that right here with us, Piper. Your father and I would be happy to have you here. We know you're going through a rough time right now," her mother insisted and looked to her father, who nodded in support.

They didn't know it but seeing the two of them together like that made her feel worse. Many things had tested their marriage, yet they were still together, in love as ever.

Piper was jealous of her parent's marriage. Why couldn't some of their magic have rubbed off on her and John?

Piper knew she'd lose her mind if she stayed any longer with her parents, but she couldn't tell them that. Instead, she was moving to Cassidy Falls, Texas. As part of the divorce settlement, John signed over a family ranch he inherited from his uncle some years ago and had never taken the time to sell. She had never been to Texas, but she was excited by the idea of a fresh start on her very own ranch.

After Piper had signed the divorce papers, she put some of her things in storage and gone to spend a few days with her parents to get them up to speed. Her parents were sweet and supportive, but they were not on board with her plans.

"Mom, I promise I'll be fine. I'll call every day and keep you updated with everything going on at the ranch," Piper said in a softer voice.

"It's okay, Eve. She's a big girl now. I'm sure she'll do fine," her father finally chipped in.

Piper gave her dad a big smile before turning to her mom, who looked resigned.

"I could send you pictures and layouts, and you can give me decorating ideas." It was a last ditch offer to win her mother's support. Thankfully, it seemed to do the trick.

"Fine, but I doubt any of the hicks will appreciate my vision!" her mother had replied in an off-hand manner. Deep down, Piper knew her mother was pleased to be included.

♡

Piper packed up the rental truck and left New York City. It would take her three to four days to drive cross country. Her parents had offered to pay for her things to be shipped over. But Piper was looking forward to the road trip. Other than their Holidays in the Catskills, her parents had never taken her anywhere as a child. Since marrying John, the farthest she'd gone from the city was their home in Jersey. It was time she saw the world. Or a little more of the U.S.A., at the very least.

As Piper drove, the city gave way to suburbs, quaint towns and villages, and wide-open spaces. Piper wasn't only shedding layers of clothing as she entered the south. She was shrugging off her old life. This was her chance to become an entirely new person. She imagined herself surrounded by horses, endless fields, and kind people who would welcome a newcomer in their midst.

When she arrived at Cassidy Falls, the warm air wasn't as sweet as she had imagined. If anything, it smelled like cow manure. At least the area around the stockyards certainly did. She chuckled and decided it was better than being assaulted by the perfume ladies at Macy's. She had it all figured out. She would head to the local diner, hire a couple of ranch hands, and get the place up and running in no time.

John's lawyer had provided her with a picture of the house. As she pulled up to the gate, she frowned. First, the gate was covered with vines and mostly rusted over. Second, the house that lay beyond it was nowhere near the pretty farmhouse in the photo. Perhaps she'd taken a wrong turn. She looked up at the awning above the gate, and her heart sank when she saw the words 'Welcome to Baker Ranch.' Sure enough, she was in the right place.

Piper climbed out of the car and walked up to the gates, wondering how she'd get inside. She started pulling out some of the vines. Her arms had started to ache when she finally managed to get the gate free. It was unlocked, and the latch was broken. She applied her weight on the first gate and pushed. The gate was heavy, and the hinges whined in protest, but she was able to open it wide enough to get the truck through. Piper was covered in sweat, her t-shirt sticking to her skin in the oppressive heat. It would take some getting used to, but she would adjust in time.

She climbed back into the truck and maneuvered to the house. Up close, the house didn't look quite as sinister as it did from the gate. She had been led to believe the ranch had been unoccupied for the last three years. The place had likely been abandoned for over a decade.

All the lower windows were boarded up, and some of the upper windows were cracked. A few had missing panes where birds had set up nests. The front door looked like it was about to fall off its hinges and onto the porch. How could Piper live there? It was no wonder John had signed it over to her without argument.

She stared at the house for a while longer and then climbed out of the truck. With her hands on her hips, she walked around the farmhouse. It didn't improve upon closer inspection. The porch had holes in it, and the paint was peeling.

Reaching for the house keys, Piper eyed the front door warily. Surely the inside of the house had to be better than the outside. She couldn't help the tears that sprung into her eyes. She had no plan 'B.' Aside from a bit of money and the stuff in her truck, this was all she had. Piper looked around in despair. John had given her a worthless piece of trash.

Her parents were right. She should have come out and looked at the ranch before dropping everything and moving on a whim. She reached for her phone to call her parents and stopped. If she told them the truth, they would ask her to come home. She would only be proving them right, that she couldn't handle being on her own.

She glanced back at all the things that were sitting in the truck. No, she would see this through. She took pictures of the ranch, gate, and the outside of the house.

She put the key in the lock and turned, with her hand bracing the door. Gingerly, she opened the door and gave a triumphant yelp when it didn't fall off its hinges. It was dark inside. She flipped a switch. The lights seemed to be working. At least the lawyer had seen to that. She took a quick tour of the house, snapped some pictures, and checked that the house had running water. It came out brown and gritty from the faucet, but it ran.

She sent the pictures to the lawyer and requested an additional amount be sent to make the place livable. The lawyer messaged her to have an estimate drawn, and they would see what could be done.

Pleased that the lawyer hadn't refused outright, Piper locked up the house and returned to the truck. It was evident that she couldn't sleep there tonight.

Piper headed towards town and got a room at the lone B&B. The owner, Millie, was a great source of information. She directed Piper to a local garage where she could buy a car and return the rental truck.

At the diner across the street, Piper asked the waitress how to find ranch hands. "You can put an ad by the front door. Maybe talk to Ben at the bar," she replied in her easy southern drawl. Piper thanked her, finished her meal, and left.

Back in her room, she sat at the desk to write her ad. She had taken a look at the bulletin board on her way out. Ads were short and sweet. She decided she should hire a ranch manager, and he would likely take care of the rest. When she was satisfied with her ad, she wrote two more. She'd place one at the feed store, in addition to one at what looked to be the local bar, and one at the diner in the morning.

Two

SAWYER SIGHED as he and his car zoomed past the 'Welcome to Cassidy Falls' sign. It still looked the same. He found it hard to believe that he had been gone for five years already. He'd left for greener pastures, intent on making it big in Nashville. Things had been going well for him. Through his job as a music producer, he'd met the beautiful Peggy-Lee Michaels. The up-and-coming singer had stolen his heart with her sad melodies and her sweet smile. They were married within six months and had been talking about starting a family when fate stepped in.

It was a chilly autumn night, he remembered. His car now stopped. The Tennessee wind blew the leaves in swirling patterns across the parking lot. The recording session hadn't gone well, and Sawyer had been late coming home. When he arrived, tired and hungry, the house was completely dark, and the front door stood wide open. He rushed into the house, calling for Peggy-Lee, but she didn't answer. It was total chaos inside, drawers overturned with their contents strewn about the room. He continued to call Peg's name, desperately searching each room for any sign of her. Sawyer prayed she had left the house and was with a neighbor.

His worst fears were realized when he found her on the kitchen floor, that fateful October night. She was lying at an odd angle, her silky blond hair fanned out in a puddle of congealing blood. He'd called to her, but she wouldn't wake up. He'd carefully checked for a pulse, reluctant to move her if she had head trauma. But she was gone. The wail he let out must have been loud enough to alert the neighbors.

He had no recollection of what had happened next, only that the police and an ambulance had arrived and taken his girl away. The days following the murder were a whirlwind of police interviews. They had gone through every inch of the house, looking for clues to what happened to Peggy-Lee. The fingerprints matched up to a known felon who was suspected of several local robberies. The break-in fit the pattern, but the criminal had never killed anyone before this case. Peggy must have caught him in the act and startled him. She had only been shot once, but the bullet had pierced her brain and killed her instantly.

Someone had found Randy's number in Sawyer's phone and called him. Sawyer spent a few weeks staying with his best friend, unable to function. He couldn't eat or sleep. He wore the same t-shirt and sweatpants for days at a time until Randy forced him to shower and change. Numbness overtook him. It was the only way he could cope. Sawyer was a shadow of his former self, with black circles under his eyes only emphasizing his weary look.

The day after the funeral, Sawyer told Randy that he was selling him his half of the recording studio and leaving town. He also knew he could never go home again. The memory of his precious songbird bleeding out on the kitchen floor would forever be tattooed into his mind.

He contacted a realtor and put the house on the market. He told Peggy-Lee's folks they could take whatever they wanted from the house and he sent them the proceeds of the sale. He didn't care what they did with his stuff. They could burn it for all he cared. There was nothing but painful memories there.

Consciously, Sawyer knew no one blamed him. But he could not handle the guilt he felt. He kept telling himself he was the reason she died. If he had come home sooner, he would have interrupted the robbery and saved his girl. They'd made off with a handful of bills and some stereo equipment, but what they'd really stolen that night was his heart. When the police caught the killer, it did nothing to help Sawyer. Nothing they did could bring back his Peggy.

All Sawyer wanted to do was forget about this tragedy. He needed to put all of this behind him and start over. But where? Sawyer got into his truck and started driving. There was no plan. He just needed to put as much space as possible between him and the place he used to call home.

He drove until he reached eastern Tennessee and found a construction job. The work was backbreaking. Long hours, low pay, but it was a good distraction from the emotional turmoil that kept him awake at night. He came to depend on sleeping pills to chase the nightmares away. When the over-the-counter meds stopped working, he convinced a doctor to prescribe him something more potent.

The stronger medication had more severe side effects. Sawyer had trouble focusing during the day and would often suffer from dizzy spells. Soon, he began to make mistakes at work. They were small things at first. Things people didn't notice or didn't care to notice. It went on like that for years. Eventually, there was an accident, and someone almost got killed. When Sawyer refused a drug test, he was fired on the spot.

Sawyer swore he would never touch a pill again. The first two weeks were the hardest, but he tried to get his old job back when the worst of the withdrawal symptoms had passed. The foreman turned him away. Unfortunately, he lived in a small town, and word had gotten out about the accident. No one would hire him.

Sawyer had nowhere to go, and he didn't have much money left. His luck had run out. Loath as he was to admit defeat, he decided it was time to go home. Sawyer needed to face his past if he ever wanted to have a future. It would be an uphill battle, but he had to try. For Peggy. She would want him to put the pieces of his life back together.

Sawyer stopped for the night at a roadside motel, just outside of his hometown. He wanted one more day to map out his game plan. He and Randy had lost touch a few years after he'd moved away. He didn't think it was right to just show up on Randy's doorstep unannounced. Sawyer's folks passed away when he was young, and his sister was married and living in California. There was no one in Cassidy Falls to roll out the red carpet and welcome him home.

The next morning, Sawyer headed to the diner for breakfast. He needed to find a place to stay and a job as soon as possible. The diner was the best place to put feelers out. He checked the bulletin board on the way in but didn't see anything interesting.

He ambled over to the counter and sat down. The waitress brought him a cup of coffee and asked what he wanted to eat. She was new and didn't recognize him. Sawyer gave her his order and sipped his coffee while he waited. The place hadn't changed at all since he'd been gone. It was after nine, and the breakfast rush was over. Folks around here came in at the crack of dawn. He saw a few moms with their tots, some old men playing checkers, and a family having breakfast before setting off on the next leg of their journey. He'd seen their van outside, packed to the gills. The bell over the door rang just then, and a petite brunette came in, ponytail swinging. She stayed only long enough to pin something to the board and went out the door. Sawyer watched her head over to the feed store next and come back out just as fast. He lost sight of her then and turned back, as his plate of food had arrived.

"Do you know if anyone's hiring?" he asked her.

She nodded at the bulletin board. "The lady who just walked out is looking for some ranch hands. She just put up an ad. You should check it out on your way out," she said, wiping down the counter.

He finished his breakfast, paid in cash, and left the diner with Piper's ad in his hands. A job as a ranch manager would be perfect. If he was lucky, they'd have accommodations on-site, and he could just move in right away.

Three

～

THE NEXT DAY, Piper woke with a sense of purpose. She had a little money put aside. She could afford to stay at the B&B for a little while until she found some people to whip the ranch into shape. All that it needed was a little elbow grease. The work would keep her mind off her failed marriage, and she'd be proud of having made it on her own.

Breakfast was included, and Piper had a lovely chat with an elderly couple passing through on their way to visit their daughter. After seeing how casual everyone was dressed yesterday, she'd put on a pair of jeans, a t-shirt, and a pair of ankle boots. While the boots weren't exactly right for ranch wear, the rest of her outfit was, judging by what others had been wearing when she'd looked around the day before. She resolved to find a pair of decent boots at the first opportunity. The last thing she needed was to meet a snake unprepared.

She headed first to the diner, then to the general store before making her way to the garage. Roger, the owner, helped her pick out a used Chevy pick-up that would handle life on a ranch. It was a far cry for the luxury S.U.V. she used to drive back in New York, but it was hers - bought and paid for with her own money. She made arrangements to have the truck delivered later that morning and headed back to the B&B.

She was crossing the street when her phone rang.

"Hello?" she answered, excited to see that it was a local number.

"Hello, ma'am. My name is Sawyer, and I'm calling about your ad," said the voice on the other end.

There seemed to be an echo. She stopped, looked at her phone, and shrugged. "Hello Sawyer, my name is Piper Baker. Do you have experience running a ranch?" she asked, as she got to the other side of the street. She stopped, once on the sidewalk, so she could give the call her full attention.

♡

"Yes, ma'am. I used to run my dad's ranch right here in Cassidy Falls," replied Sawyer, staring at her as she paced down the sidewalk.

She was clearly not a local. The ad had mentioned the job was out at Baker Ranch. If it was the same one he remembered, the place had gone by the wayside around the time he had left. He couldn't recall the owner's name, only that he had died without any kin to take over.

"How long ago was that Sawyer?" she asked shrewdly. She was inspecting her nails, as if wondering whether or not she'd chipped one.

"It was over ten years ago, ma'am. I've been living in Nashville for a while and only recently came back to town," he said, accentuating his drawl.

"Do you have any references I could check? When would you be available for an interview?"

"Sure, I have references," he said. He'd have to call Randy and set something up. "And I can meet you right away if you're available."

She checked her watch. She would need to show Sawyer the ranch so he'd know what he was getting into before agreeing to work for her.

"I could meet you at the ranch in about thirty minutes. Would that suit you?" Piper asked.

He debated letting her know he was standing right across the street. She was a city girl. Those designer jeans and boots didn't fool him.

There was nothing casual about this woman. She would likely freak out if she found out he'd been staring at her for the past ten minutes.

"That'll do me fine, ma'am. See you then," Sawyer drawled and ended the call.

He waited until she'd gone into the B&B before getting into his truck. He'd head over to the ranch right away to get the lay of the land. That way, he'd have a few suggestions handy when they finally met.

When he got to Baker Ranch, Sawyer couldn't believe his luck. This place was perfect. He took in the creaking gate, the dilapidated house, the rotting mass of barn, and whistled. He would be here forever. It was far away from town and from the memories that still haunted him.

A quick look at the fields told him he had his work cut out for him. Rubbing his hands together, he reached into his jacket. He pulled out a notebook, jotting down a list of priority jobs to be done.

The Baker Ranch used to be the largest in Cassidy Falls while Old Timothy was alive. A ranch this big was challenging to manage and needed dozens of hands to keep it afloat. After Tim died, Sawyer assumed no one could take up the responsibility, and his relatives just let the place fall into disrepair. Now, years later, this sophisticated lady was looking to reopen the place.

Sawyer couldn't imagine how much money it would cost to get it up and running again. He needed to make calculations because he was sure she'd want to know the price right away.

The gate was open when he arrived at the ranch, and he slowly drove through them. The property was overgrown with weeds breaking through the pavement and crowding the pastures. Sawyer was amazed that the buildings were still standing after years of neglect. The gravel driveway crunched under his boots as he stepped out of his truck. He walked around the house's exterior and jotted down suggestions in two lists: safety and upgrades. The first list detailed the repairs that were needed to make the place livable. The second one had suggestions to make things enjoyable.

The inside wasn't as bad as he expected. The joists were sturdy, and there was no apparent water damage in either bathroom. The electricity worked but would need to be upgraded soon to handle the construction equipment. The kitchen was passable, although Mrs. Baker would probably want to spruce it up eventually.

Sawyer checked the staff quarters next. The sink and shower hardware was corroded but could easily be replaced. The rest of the issues could be fixed with new sheetrock and a fresh coat of paint. Luckily, it wouldn't take long to get this up and running.

The barn was a little iffy, but the rest of the buildings seemed like they were in decent shape. Sawyer made a few phone calls to get pricing and leaned against his truck while writing down figures. Hopefully, he wouldn't scare off Mrs. Baker with his estimate.

Four

PIPER WAS PLEASANTLY surprised to see that Sawyer had beat her to the ranch. It showed initiative.

She held out her hand and he shook it. "Eager to begin?" she asked, for lack of a better greeting.

"Just a bit," Sawyer answered with a smile. He was cringing inside for not being able to come up with a better response.

"Sawyer, I had a speech ready on how important it is for you to know what you're getting into," she said as she waved around, "but it seems you've already had a chance to look things over. What's your prognosis, then?"

"The way I see it," he said, "there are two ways you can go about this. You can tear down the buildings on the property now and rebuild them. Or you repair what you can and upgrade them later."

"Which do you suggest?"

Sawyer handed Piper a price list that broke down the cost of materials and labor for repair versus rebuilding. "These buildings have decent bones." He kicked the side of the house for emphasis. "It would lower your upfront costs to repair what's here. And you wouldn't have to deal with construction companies and permits."

Piper glanced at the sheet of paper and made some mental calculations. Depending on how much money she convinced John's lawyer to send her, she might be able to rebuild right away, but that would likely tap out her funds. Who knew how long it would take to have a steady income again?

"I agree," she said. "When can you start?"

Sawyer had been expecting resistance, outrage, or downright hysterics. Clearly, this woman had no idea how to haggle. The fact that she trusted him blindly made him feel protective of her. Someone needed to look out for her interests.

"I could start today if you'd like."

"Great, let's have lunch and discuss the plans."

Sawyer smiled and thrust out his hand. "You've got yourself a deal, Mrs. Baker."

"Call me Piper," she replied before turning on her heels.

They ate lunch at the diner where Piper had posted her ad. With the lunch crowd gone, it was quiet enough where they could have a conversation. The waitress smiled as she poured each of them a cup of water.

"What'll ya have?"

Piper looked up from her menu. "I'll have a cheeseburger – medium – and a large cherry soda."

It was nice to see a woman who didn't live off salad. Sawyer turned to the waitress. "Can I please have the barbeque burger and a chocolate milkshake, ma'am?"

"Sure thing, sweetheart."

Piper pulled the folded piece of paper out of her pocket and flattened it out on the table. "I think we start with the staff quarters," she suggested. "That way, you could move right in, and we'd be able to lodge the farmhands as we hire them."

"I think that's a mighty good idea." Even though Piper was too trusting, she had good ideas. Sawyer was hopeful that things were finally working in his favor.

"I'll put money into an account so you can order workers and materials."

"It'll take a few days to get the repairs up and running, but I can hire people to begin cleanup right away."

"Excellent," Piper said. Her eyes sparkled with excitement. To his surprise he found himself noticing how pretty she was when she smiled.

Sawyer considered asking her how she ended up with Old Timothy's ranch but thought better of it. He didn't feel right prying into her personal life, especially when they had just met. Still, he was curious.

After lunch, they went their separate ways but planned to meet early the next morning. They needed to work out the details of phase one and decide how many people they should hire. Sawyer looked forward to working on a ranch again and its possibilities. It had been a while since he had this much responsibility, and he wanted to prove to himself that he was worthy of the trust Piper put in him. Sawyer hoped his wife was looking down on him and that he made her proud.

Sawyer found a cheap room to rent on a week-to-week basis. It wasn't much, but it had a bed and a small closet to store his clothing. He had to share a bathroom down the hall with one other tenant, but the guy worked nights as a security guard, so their schedules didn't conflict. The old lady who owned the house had only lived in Cassidy Falls a few years, so she didn't know Sawyer's past. It was easier that way. He wasn't ready to share his story.

The bed was comfortable, but Sawyer still slept fitfully. Familiarity brought down his guard, and he wasn't ready for the onslaught of emotions that plagued his dreams. Morning came, and Sawyer shook the cobwebs from his mind. He was exhausted, but it was nothing a little coffee couldn't cure. Now, if it could only fix the ache in his heart, he might have a chance.

Instead of dwelling on his pain, Sawyer shoved it to the furthest recesses of his mind and buried himself in his work. The quicker he got the staff quarters ready, the sooner he'd be able to move there. Once he was settled in, his days would be filled with projects that would push him to the point of exhaustion, hopefully giving him dreamless nights.

Five

WITHIN A MONTH OF HIRING SAWYER, Piper realized she had made a great decision. Work began immediately, and he quickly hired several people to fix up the staff quarters. It only took a week to get the building livable, and they could stay there while they finished the rest of the improvements. There were six bedrooms with private bathrooms, a kitchen, and a large common room when it was complete. As a thank you for their hard work, Piper gifted them a used pool table and a large screen T.V.

With that out of the way, the staff was able to do some work on the house. The place was not fully renovated yet, but at least she could move out of the B&B. Eventually, she would like to redo the kitchen completely. But that was a project that was best left to when she had a positive income.

Piper was happy about the new developments at the ranch. Things were coming together much faster than she expected. She threw herself into cleaning and organizing the ranch house. The downstairs had a rustic feel that she complemented with items she found at local thrift shops.

Cassidy Falls didn't have any designer shops or fancy boutiques, but Piper was amazed at what she found with her limited budget.

She treated herself to a few pieces of new furniture to make it feel like a cozy place to stay. Her favorite piece was the super comfortable brown leather couch. The curved arms and rivet details pulled the living room together. She spent a lot of time curled up with a novel enjoying the warmth of the fire.

She painted the bedroom seafoam green. It was serene and made her think of a relaxing beach vacation. Sheer white curtains hung from the canopy of her four-poster bed, and the mattress was topped with a plush layer of padding. Despite the unfinished state of the house, Piper felt like she was staying in a luxury hotel.

The farmhands kept her busy. Even though Piper hired Sawyer as the ranch manager, ultimately, she was the boss. She hadn't realized she would need to feed them such large meals every day. Eventually, they got a routine going. She'd get up early and put the coffee on. She'd found one of those industrial coffee machines, the kind you saw at conventions. At first, she'd gone the continental route, leaving fruit and fresh-baked muffins out for them to grab. Sawyer explained that they needed more sustenance in the morning.

Cooking for six people every morning was more work than she anticipated. Piper was used to making food for two. She winced at the thought.

Sawyer woke up early to help, and each morning they cooked huge trays of omelets and bacon. It was nice to have help; they made a good team. Piper put the food out with the fruit, muffins, and coffee. With the addition of juice, toast, and jams, she felt it was a healthy breakfast, and the farmhands were happier. After breakfast, Piper often made stew and left it in the slow cooker to simmer all day. The kitchen smelled wonderful from morning till night.

The barn wasn't as sturdy as they initially thought, so it needed to be rebuilt entirely. Luckily, Sawyer handled the permits and inspections. Since they were rebuilding from the original plans, they could do most of the work themselves, saving a lot of money.

"How were you able to find the plans?" Piper asked. She unrolled the plans and spread them across the table.

"They were filed with the town."

"Great work. Thank you."

Sawyer blushed. "Just doing my job, ma'am."

"When are you going to start calling me by my first name?" Piper teased.

"I'm just trying to be respectful."

"Ma'am makes me feel old."

"Sorry, ma'am, I mean Piper."

The work on the barn continued steadily, and Piper grew used to the constant sounds of hammers pounding and the buzz of the electric saw. It became familiar, a reminder of all they accomplished. It gave her some stability after all she had been through recently.

As time progressed, Pier and Sawyer formed a casual friendship. After Piper had satellite T.V. installed in the house and staff quarters, they often spent time together watching home improvement shows and crime dramas. It was a pleasant divergence from nights spent alone sobbing into her pillow.

Although Piper was over John, she still felt a profound sense of loss. He threw her aside so easily. Her self-esteem had plummeted since the night he confessed his affair. She wondered if something was wrong with her. *Besides being barren*, she thought bitterly. The lingering rejection caused Piper to drink more than usual. She soon replaced the strength she got from watching the ranch improve with liquid courage.

This new coping mechanism began to affect her work. She avoided going downstairs first thing in the morning, leaving Sawyer to manage breakfast on his own. He never complained, though. Piper knew how lucky she was to have such a loyal employee. The guilt of her neglect grew, and she found herself avoiding Sawyer during the day. She felt the widening distance between them, but it never affected his work. In fact, he worked harder than ever.

Piper tried to make up for her behavior, when she wasn't in bed, by preparing extravagant dinners for the crew. She's made roasts and baked pies in hopes of nullifying what she saw as flaws. Piper had always been a people-pleaser. Asking John about the affair was the first time she had ever confronted him about anything. When she ignored her mom's insistence on living with them instead of moving to the farm, Piper thought she had broken the pattern. But old habits die hard. And she fell back to her routine as soon as she thought people were displeased with her. It made her feel weak. She knew she should deal with this, but for now, she let herself wallow in her sorrow.

Six

SAWYER COULD TELL that the dark patches under Piper's eyes were more than just a lack of sleep. She handled the schedule fine in the beginning, so why was she struggling now? Something had changed. She had a haunted look that worried him.

The handful of times Sawyer saw her that week, he subtly tried to ask if everything was okay, and every time she would tell him everything was fine. If he asked too many questions about how she was feeling, Piper promptly shut him down. The extravagant dinners also worried him. They were delicious, but she was doling out more money than she needed to spend. That money would be better spent on making improvements to the ranch. There was still tons of work that needed to get done to get the ranch ready to reopen.

They were never particularly close, but he considered her a friend. Neither of them was all that forthcoming about their past, which helped preserve the boss-employee boundaries. They kept their conversations to television shows and the ranch. That was more than enough to give them things to talk about, with all the recent improvements.

One night, Sawyer stayed late in the house to finish washing dishes. Piper came downstairs. He was surprised when she joined him at the sink. He could see she'd been crying. Wet streaks still stained her face.

The room was filled with the sound of running water that was occasionally joined by her sniffles. Without a word, he handed her his handkerchief.

"Thank you," she whispered.

The forlorn sound of her voice broke Sawyer's heart. He knew that feeling. He knew what despair could do to a person. He turned to her, about to ask if she wanted to talk, but before he could say anything, he was taken aback by the composed smile on her face.

"Would you like to join me on the porch for a beer after we finish?"

"Sure," he said casually.

They toasted to the upcoming reopening. Sawyer studied Piper carefully. She acted as if nothing was wrong, and she hadn't hidden away for the past few weeks. They sat quietly, the sound of crickets filling the void between them.

"I can't believe we got the ranch up to speed so fast," she said, taking a swig of beer.

The silence was broken, and it startled Sawyer. "It's taken four months. I wouldn't call that fast," he replied, an amused smile on his lips.

"We're further along than I thought we'd be at this point. The barn is finished, so I'll be able to get some cattle soon."

"You gotta wait until the heat and electricity are in," Sawyer explained. "It may not get all that cold at night this far south, but even cattle get cranky when it's dark and chilly."

Piper laughed. "I'm going to grab more beer. Do you want some?"

"Nah, I'm good."

Another three beers relaxed Piper, and she became chattier. "So, Sawyer, tell me, why are you here?" she asked.

"I live here," he said, gesturing at the staff quarters.

She shifted in her seat, almost knocking over the beer she placed on the deck. "Don't sass me, Sawyer. Why did you come back to Cassidy Falls?"

Sawyer stared at the whirls in the wood below him and took a moment to compose himself. With a heavy sigh, he looked up and met Piper's curious gaze. The intense focus felt like being blinded by a spotlight, but maybe she would open up to him if he shared some of his life.

"Five years ago, my wife was murdered," he began. "I was working late, and a burglar broke into the house. We had only been married for six months. If I hadn't been late-" Sawyer paused for a minute to steady himself. "Anyway, I just felt like it was time to come home."

Piper listened without saying a word or making a huge deal about his story. She simply said, "I'm sorry that happened to you."

It was the best thing she could say. Sawyer couldn't have handled her pity. He'd enjoyed the respect she gave him, and she trusted his skills and knowledge. It felt good to be relied upon, needed. Piper believed in him when no one else had for a long time.

He was about to ask for her own story when he noticed she'd gone silent. Looking over at her, he saw her head lolling. She'd fallen asleep in the rocker.

Sawyer debated getting a blanket and leaving her there. She wouldn't be attacked by wild animals overnight, but there was no telling what some of the hands might do if they had too much to drink and found a pretty little thing like her passed out on the front porch.

He scooped her up and took her inside. He hadn't been on the second floor since he repaired the stairs. They no longer creaked as he took them two at a time and headed toward the master bedroom.

He placed Piper on the bed, took off her shoes, and draped her with the plush blanket he found on the back of a chaise by the window. She looked more peaceful in sleep, with her stress melting away. He hoped her dreams were more pleasant than his. On impulse, he brushed the hair from her face and placed a light kiss on her forehead.

Seven

PIPER WOKE up in bed the next day with a hangover. She must have drunk more than she thought, and skipping dinner didn't help. Piper didn't remember going up to bed last night and guessed that Sawyer must have carried her there. She hoped she hadn't made a complete fool of herself. He was her employee, after all.

She knew she should find him and apologize. Still, she was embarrassed about falling asleep immediately after his gut-wrenching story. Sure, her divorce was emotionally draining, but losing the love of your life to such a horrific crime was unimaginable. Piper wanted to do something to make up for her rudeness.

After getting dressed, she popped a pain killer and headed downstairs. The smell of breakfast caught up with her midway down the stairs, but the kitchen was empty when she got there. The men had neatly stacked the dishes next to the sink.

She poured herself a cup and was thankful she'd dodged a bullet. She still felt a little off; the dishes could wait. She went to sit on the back porch to watch the sunrise. Though she'd slept in later than usual, the sun was barely over the horizon as she sank into the soft cushions of the lounger and promptly fell asleep.

A hand on her shoulder startled her from her nap. Piper jolted upright. Sawyer stood over her blocking the harsh rays of the midday sun.

"Whoa, hey, it's just me," he said and pulled up a chair and sat next to her. "Are you feeling okay?"

An awkward silence stretched between them while Piper thought about how to answer his question. It would be easier to lie, but she knew he would see right through it. "I feel like hell," she finally said.

"You look it," Sawyer replied. "I mean, um-"

"It's okay. I'm sure I do."

"You need to take better care of yourself."

"I will." If he only knew how bad it was, he probably wouldn't say that out loud. Piper appreciated his caring nature, though, and didn't want him to worry.

"Oh, and I took care of the dishes from this morning."

"You are an absolute angel. Thank you."

"Aw, shucks. It was nothing."

Piper chose her next words carefully. "I'm sorry about falling asleep on you last night. I was exhausted."

"It's fine. I was just rambling anyway."

"No, it was rude of me. I shouldn't have put you in the position of dragging my lazy butt to bed, and I'd like to make it up to you. I can cook you something special. What's your favorite dish?"

"You don't have to," he said. "Although I do miss my mom's home-made macaroni and cheese."

"Perfect. Come up to the house for dinner at seven."

The al dente pasta slid from the colander into the cheese sauce. Piper stirred until every last piece was coated and dumped the mixture into a ceramic baking pan. She topped it with herbed breadcrumbs and put it in the oven. The clock read six-thirty, which gave her angel food loaf plenty of time to cool.

Piper hummed to herself as she sliced strawberries and whipped heavy cream. She felt lighter on her feet, unfettered, as she lost herself in the motions of cooking. She always enjoyed it and was pleased to make something special for someone again.

The earthy smell of cheese permeated the farmhouse. Sawyer closed his eyes for a moment and let the childhood memories float through his mind. His mama's apron powdered with flour, the excitement at the dinner table as they shared stories of their day, dad's hearty laugh. They were old memories but still sharp in his mind, as if they were yesterday.

"Is that you, Sawyer?" Piper called from the kitchen.

"Yeah, it's me."

"Dinner just came out of the oven. I'll meet you in the dining room."

A new tablecloth covered the wooden table. It had been bought recently, still stiff with the deep creases of being folded for a long time. In contrast, the dishes were chipped and faded from years of use.

Piper wore green oven mitts and carried a small, square baking dish into the room. She placed it in the center of the table and spooned a heaping serving on top of Sawyer's plate. She returned to the kitchen to retrieve a chilled bottle of Riesling and poured them each a glass.

Sawyer waited for Piper to be seated before he raised his glass. "To the Baker Ranch."

"To you, for working so hard," she added.

Sawyer blushed a little at the compliment. He hadn't felt proud of himself in a long time. Steam rose from the dish, warming his face, and his anticipation built as he brought the first bite to his lips.

"Be careful. It's hot," Piper said.

Sawyer blew across the forkful of pasta and opened his mouth. The sauce was creamy, and a mixture of buttery and nutty flavors burst on his tongue. He looked up and saw Piper watching for his reaction, and he nodded enthusiastically.

After a few bites, Sawyer took a sip of the wine.

It wasn't his usual drink of choice, but the sweetness paired perfectly with the salty dish. He was quiet while he ate, too busy enjoying each morsel of food.

The cake that followed was light and airy. The strawberries were ripe and sweet, and the fresh whipped cream tasted terrific. "Did you make this all yourself?" Sawyer asked after swallowing the last bite.

Piper nodded. "I used to have a lot more free time," she said bitterly and poured another glass of wine. "I always cooked for my husband . . . ex-husband."

"I'm sorry." Sawyer waited to see if she would continue.

"At first, things were great, ya know. We were happy. John and I were excited to start a family, but as time passed, we realized something was wrong."

Piper drained her glass and refilled it again. Sawyer watched as the cheerfulness from the beginning of the evening sunk into misery. He considered excusing himself to go to bed, but she needed to get this out of her system. He hoped that confiding in him might lighten her load.

The alcohol loosened her tongue. "We took every test and tried every treatment. We even tried in-vitro, but nothing worked. It turns out my eggs aren't viable."

Sawyer felt uncomfortable hearing the intimate details of Piper's life. He was sure she wouldn't divulge them if she were sober. "Let me help you clear the dishes."

As Sawyer stood, Piper slammed her hand on the table. "The bastard cheated on me." Her voice was rough, and tears welled up in her eyes. "He knocked up some floozy. Can you believe that?"

Sawyer hesitated, unsure of how to handle the situation. When she began to sob, he tentatively placed a hand on her shoulder. "It's going to be okay." He pulled her up from her seat, and she buried her face against his shoulder. Sawyer awkwardly patted her back.

After a few minutes, the crying ceased, and Piper lifted her head. Her eyes widened in realization, and she pulled away from Sawyer. "I'm sorry," she whispered and fled upstairs.

Sawyer watched her retreat but didn't follow. On some level, Sawyer understood what she was going through. They had both lost people they loved, even if the circumstances were drastically different. And they had both turned to substance abuse to dampen the pain. Although Sawyer resisted the urge to drown out his dreams with sleeping pills, he knew he was only one bad day away from relapsing.

Piper was right smack in the middle of addiction. But maybe with a bit of coaxing, she would consider stopping. It was easier to beat it if you had some support. Sawyer planned to talk to her about it tomorrow.

After he finished cleaning the kitchen, he headed back to his room for the night. There was a note slipped under the door, the fourth one this week. Sawyer grabbed it and tore the envelope open. He read the messy handwriting and shoved the note angrily into his pocket. Things were good while they lasted, but he knew it was time to move on.

Eight

PIPER OPENED her eyes and immediately closed them. The sunlight filtering through the window felt like hundreds of tiny knives stabbing her brain. She felt worse than yesterday. Nausea caused bile to creep up Piper's throat, and she grabbed a nearby trash can. She retched, but nothing came up. Her entire body ached, and she felt exhausted, so she grabbed the covers and pulled them over her head. A few more minutes of sleep would help her feel better.

A few minutes turned into hours, and it was already past lunchtime when Piper woke up again. She rolled out of bed and trudged downstairs, not even bothering to change out of yesterday's clothes. She was looking forward to a hot cup of coffee, but the carafe was empty, and there were no breakfast dishes in the sink. In fact, it looked like no one even made breakfast that morning. The ranch was also eerily quiet.

Piper poked her head out the front door to see what was happening. Some workers were milling around in front of the staff quarters, and they whispered amongst themselves as she approached.

"Why isn't anyone working? Is everything okay?"

One of the carpenters, Tim, stepped forward. "We finished this morning's task list. We're waiting to see what Sawyer needs us to do next."

"Where's Sawyer?"

"I don't rightly know, ma'am. He wasn't around this morning. We figured he was out getting supplies, but he hasn't come back. I tried calling him, but there's no answer."

Piper took a breath and tried to shake the cobwebs from her mind. "Okay, go take a quick peek in his room and see if he forgot his phone, and I'll call around to see if anyone has seen him. He probably got caught up helping someone. You know how he is."

He nodded and headed into the building. Piper pulled her phone out of her pocket and called the lumber yard. Sawyer hadn't been there, or the hardware store, or the diner. Fear tightened her chest as she imagined something horrible happening to him. Without waiting for an answer from Tim, she took off.

Adrenaline coursed through Piper, clearing her headache but making her nausea worse. She rushed into the house, grabbed her keys, and tore out of the driveway. As she headed into town, she tried calling the hospital. No one was there that fit Sawyer's description. That worried her even more, so she stopped every so often to check ditches and fields, but she didn't see his car. She drove around asking anyone she ran into for the next hour, but no one had seen Sawyer all day. She even called all her vendors a second time, asking them to reach out to her if they saw him.

When she arrived home, Piper exited the car, hoping that Sawyer was already there but was disappointed when she didn't see his truck. She hurried to the staff quarters where Tim was waiting for her, looking anxious. "Any news?"

Tim frowned. "He's gone."

Piper thought she must have misheard him. "What do you mean he's gone?"

"His room's been cleared out," he explained. "Looks like he packed up and took off."

Piper adamantly shook her head. "He wouldn't do that."

Tim shrugged. "It happens all the time. Other ranch owners see good work and make better offers."

"He wouldn't do that," she said again, trying to convince herself more than him.

"What should we do now, ma'am?"

"Take the rest of the day off. You're welcome to use the kitchen to make dinner." Piper didn't know what else to tell him.

Tim politely tipped his hat and gathered up the other men. They went into the house to eat, and Piper walked into the staff quarters. In the common room, pool cues lay across the table of an abandoned game, and a few empty beers lined the kitchen counter. Piper hadn't been in here in a while, preferring to give her staff some privacy.

There must have been some mistake. Sawyer wouldn't just take off without an explanation. In the short amount of time she'd known him, he had shown himself to be loyal and honorable. Even if a competitor offered him more money, she would have beat that offer. Piper went into his room, and it was just as empty as Tim described. Sawyer's clothes were gone, and the bathroom was cleaned of toiletries. She even crawled around on the floor, searching to see if he'd left a note. Maybe it had tumbled under the desk or something. As she looked, she knew her efforts were futile. If he'd needed to take care of something, he would have called or texted her.

Piper went back to her room and tried calling Sawyer, but it went straight to voicemail. She was about to try again so she could leave a message when she remembered what had happened the night before. She drank too much and embarrassed herself again. Even worse, she shared the most private details of her life with someone she's only known for a short time. That must have made him uncomfortable, so much so that he didn't want to work for her anymore.

Piper knew she messed up royally this time. Maybe she was the problem; Sawyer had left her for greener pastures, just like her husband. And just like with her husband, there was no way to fix things. What was she supposed to do now?

Nine

~

PIPER ALLOWED the ranch hands to take the rest of the day off, then she sat on the porch with a beer. She knew she had embarrassed herself. Why else would Sawyer leave without so much as a word to her or the ranch hands? It left her feeling perplexed. She thought they had become friends over the last few months, that they had mutual respect.

'*Friends don't do that to each other*' she thought, taking another swig of her beer. The ranch still had a fair amount of work that needed doing before becoming a working ranch. She didn't know which way to turn next. She spent the rest of the day trying to find odd jobs to do, but she could not find the motivation to do any of it. Eventually, she settled in front of the T.V. with a bottle of wine.

She woke the next morning to find the wine bottle half-empty on the floor; she had fallen asleep on the couch. Her neck hurt from sleeping in an awkward position, and her head ached a little. Well, she'd had worse hangovers. She told herself to get up and start the day.

The sun shone beautifully outside sending, shades of yellow and orange cast around the room. "Today is going to be different. I can't depend on anyone but myself. No more pity parties. Do what needs to be done," she said out loud to herself. She headed upstairs, showered, dressed, and feeling more human, she went to start breakfast for her staff.

"What do you want us to do today, ma'am?" asked one of the ranch hands when they came in to eat.

She stalled for a second, not knowing how to answer. "Nothing, for now. You have all been working so hard. Why not take the day off? I'm going to go out and find Sawyer's replacement." She smiled. He tipped his hat in thanks.

After breakfast, Piper headed to her room and penned a handful of new ads that she planned to scatter around town. '*Maybe Sawyer leaving is the kick in the butt I need to get myself straight again,*' she thought, as she jumped in her truck and drove into town.

It was a scorching day, hotter than Piper had felt since arriving to Texas. Well, she wasn't going to let the blistering heat stop her. She headed from store to store and to the diner, cheerfully saying hello to anyone who would listen. Piper liked the fact that everyone in town seemed so friendly. She spent the day gathering a few more supplies, the few that she knew were needed so she could at least give her staff jobs to do until she found a new ranch manager.

Later that night, she cooked dinner for everyone but ate alone in the dining room, reassessing her situation and organizing her thoughts. She needed a shift in mindset. She no longer wanted to drown her sorrows and cry herself to sleep. She had a ranch to build.

Her parents' words rang in her ears, and John and Sawyer's departure from her life flashed in front of her eyes. She was alone, but she would not let that stop her. She had set out to make a new life for herself. She intended to do it herself. This meant getting there by any means necessary. She spent her evening going over the plans Sawyer had left behind, trying her best to make sense of it all. From his scribbled notes she created, what she felt was a reasonable list of work that needed to be done in the following days.

That night was the first night in a while where she didn't go to sleep drunk.

A week passed, and she was running out of jobs to give the ranch hands. Unfortunately, no one had replied to her ad. An all too familiar feeling of dread and self-doubt gave her a sick feeling in the pit of her stomach. Rather than allow herself to spiral down again, she decided to take action. She told her staff to tend to the fields on the far side of the ranch just past the barn, and she headed back into town.

"If no one is answering my ad, I will hunt someone down myself. I'm not coming back without a new manager," she said with a newfound spirit, as she drove once again back into town, singing along with the radio.

She spent the better part of her day making inquiries, but she couldn't get a straight answer from anyone. People seemed to purposely avoid her or give her nonsense excuses for why they couldn't help her. Puzzled, she racked her brain trying to remember if she had upset or offended anyone, but her mind drew a blank. She hadn't interacted much with anyone in town, spending most of her time rebuilding the ranch. Defeat set back in, and the wine sitting at home on the kitchen counter called her name.

Piper went to bed that night the same way she had many nights before, full of a mix of wine and beer. As a result, she slept so deeply she didn't hear the commotion going on outside. Instead, she awoke abruptly, coughing from the acrid smell of smoke. She assumed the ranch hands had burnt breakfast. She had woken up enough mornings feeling rough enough not to bother with cooking for the staff. In recent days, they'd learned quickly to fend for themselves.

Next to her bed, sat a bottle of water and a bottle of aspirin. She took her painkillers and headed to the bathroom to shower. Once dressed, she headed downstairs, the smell of burning wood getting stronger. She was coughing again by the time she made it to the front door. This was no burnt breakfast. Mystified and starting to panic, Piper headed outside to see the ranch hands slumped on the porch looking tired and defeated. Their faces and clothes were covered in soot and dust. They barely looked up as she came out.

"Ma'am, we have some bad news." One started taking off his hat as he spoke to her.

'More?" she said impatiently, the pained look on his face stabbing at her. "Sorry, I didn't mean to sound so harsh. What happened?" she asked.

The hands looked at one another uneasily. The one doing the talking grimaced and nodded toward the outbuildings. "Follow me."

She followed him across the ranch and froze when she was met with the charred remains of her barn. Months of hard work down the drain. She felt the tears well in her eyes. "How?...when?" she stammered, struggling to hide the catch in her throat, wondering how she'd been able to sleep through such a thing.

"We don't know, we smelled smoke and came out. It was pretty early. The whole thing was ablaze. We managed to put it out not long before you came down. Thankfully it hadn't spread to anywhere else on the property," he replied.

She couldn't figure out what had happened; the barn had nothing inside that could cause a fire. It mostly housed a collection of wooden tools and bags of feed she had managed to get at a discount, things she was storing for when she finally bought her cattle. "What do I do now?" she asked, more for herself than anything,

"I don't know, ma'am," came the unwanted response.

Ten

NOAH MARTINEZ HAD WATCHED the fire burn from his bedroom window. So sad that such a tragic thing could happen to the lovely brunette who had just moved in on the neighboring ranch. The fact he could see the fire from his ranch meant there was no way anything could have survived. So Sad. He almost called the fire department, but from the look of things, the hands had gotten it under control easy enough.

Since the downfall of Baker Ranch all those years prior, the success of his ranch had become unmatched. There were plenty of other ranches around the small town he called home, but his had been the most extensive and most successful. Noah primarily raised cattle for meat, but lately he'd branched out into breeding prime stock for bull riding. And, even more recently, he'd started breeding prize-winning horses. His cattle won awards in local shows, gaining local respect, and an excellent bank balance. He wanted things to stay that way.

He had yet to meet his new neighbor but often found himself wondering how such a young woman, who, from what he had heard, was a city girl, planned on running such a vast ranch with little to no experience. It was an intriguing thought.

That night he slept deeply.

Now, he sat on the back porch of his farmhouse in the old rocking chair that once belonged to his father. He watched the sunrise with a glass of whiskey and a cigar. He knew the cigar he smoked was an illegal Cuban import, but he had connections, and rules were meant for people other than him. The sound of a truck engine disturbed his moment of peace, but he stayed where he sat. His ranch hand, Job Hernandez, would see to whomever it was.

After a few more moments soaking up the morning sun, he heard a faint voice that sounded like a woman. Could it be his new neighbor come to call? He strode inside and met Job, who was inviting Piper in at the front door.

"Good morning little miss, how may we help you?" he asked with a smile that spanned his entire face.

The young girl looked troubled but smiled back anyway. "Hi there, I'm Piper from Baker Ranch. There was a fire, I hope the embers didn't travel over to your land. Do you mind if I take a look around?" she asked.

Job shot Noah a cautious look, but Job always was a funny old sort. "Not at all." Noah offered her his hand. "Allow me to introduce myself, I'm Noah Martinez. It's a pleasure to finally meet my new neighbor. If you follow me, little miss, we will inspect together." He grinned.

They walked out the back of his farmhouse and headed off in the direction where their lands met. As they drew closer, the charred remains of the barn were clearly visible from his property line. The fire had been put out, but the smoke was still thick in the air. "Oh my, you are in a bit of a pickle now, aren't you? I'm so sorry little miss; that truly is a tragedy. A barn that size will cost a buck and a half to fix. I hope you have the funds," he said, keeping a close eye on her reaction.

The young woman stood eyeing the fence line between their properties. He hoped she didn't notice how he had a little more land on his side of the fence than maybe he had a right to. Of course, people rarely knew where their property lines were without an assayer getting involved.

She tried to hide that his words cut deep, turning to smile sweetly back at him. "Thank you for showing me around. I'm glad your property wasn't damaged. I have no idea what caused the fire."

Noah saw an opportunity and ran with it. "Well, excuse me for being so bold miss, but you don't seem the type who has a lot of experience in these matters. You will be surprised as to what can cause a fire in these here parts. The sun, hay stored wet. Something as simple as that can have catastrophic results."

The young woman let her gaze drop to the floor, clearly agitated.

"Oh, I am sorry little miss, I didn't mean to offend you."

"No, it's fine. I'm a tough cookie. I will rebuild," she replied with confidence, straightening up and smiling back. Her resilience intrigued Noah. Maybe she wasn't as stupid as he thought.

Noah invited Piper on a tour of the rest of his ranch so that she would see how a ranch should be run and hoped it would make her realize she was out of her depth. His aim was simple. He needed to make her see this was not the life for her. Noah showed her his two stables filled with his prize-winning horses. Then, he showed her his herd of cattle. Every so often, he casually dropped expenses into the conversation, quickly brushing past the numbers. He was planting a seed.

He ended the tour with the paddock on the furthest end of the ranch where his prized possession, a black Texas Longhorn, grazed proudly. He couldn't help feeling pleased with himself when the young woman took a step back when she locked eyes with the beast. She was very obviously intimidated by its size and how fearsome it looked.

"Mr. Martinez, your ranch is beautiful, thank you so much for the tour, but I should go." Her smile was tremulous.

"Really? So soon? I'll tell you what, come by for dinner tonight. Think of it as a welcome to Texas," he said.

After a moment of thought, she agreed.

At eight o'clock precisely, there was a knock on the door. Piper had arrived right on time. Noah had instructed Job to show Piper to the dining room. He allowed her to sit alone for a moment before he entered with a bottle of whiskey and two glasses. "I'm so glad you came. Dinner will be ready shortly. I hope you like fish." He smiled, placing a glass in front of her and filling it up.

"Thank you for having me, and yes, I love fish. You have a lovely home," she smiled back tentatively, looking at the glass with a somewhat dubious expression.

"Sorry, I don't have any wine, my wife drank it. I prefer the hard stuff." He placed the bottle down on the table between them and took a seat.

"Whiskey is fine, thank you," she replied, slowly taking a sip.

They sat making small talk over dinner. Noah was a good cook. Salmon being his specialty, he had chosen it as the dish for the evening. Piper seemed to like his cooking, he felt, as he had to try hard to drag a conversation from her. After dinner, he brought out a vanilla cheesecake topped with fresh raspberries. She exclaimed in delight when he set it before her, relaxing as the evening progressed.

"Dinner was beautiful, thank you." She smiled as they left the dining room and headed for the living room.

Noah set a roaring fire and poured her another glass of whiskey.

"I really shouldn't, I'm driving home."

"Oh, one more won't hurt," he insisted.

After her second glass, she became more talkative and seemed more willing to answer his questions. In order to gain her trust, he answered her questions just as freely. He told her how the ranch had been in his family for years, how his children were all grown and living in Europe, and talked, with some encouragement, about how his wife had left him recently, after twenty-five years of marriage.

Of course, none of it was true.

His story seemed to work, as she told him everything he needed to know.

Eleven

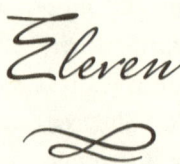

PIPER FELT a little more at ease since meeting Noah. Finding out he had experienced a similar situation to herself with relationships, and the fact that he ran a successful ranch, made her believe she could still do this.

Noah was a polite older gentleman in his early sixties but could easily pass for early fifties. He was short, with salt and pepper hair, and a short beard and handlebar mustache that was now completely white with age. She thought she had finally found a friend, someone to trust, and someone she could turn to whenever she had questions about running a ranch. Someone who obviously knew what he was doing and perhaps had connections he wouldn't mind sharing with Piper.

Yes, while he was all too eager to offer guidance and advice, she couldn't ignore the seed of doubt that was starting to grow. Noah was right about something that had been bothering her lately. Running a ranch was expensive and getting the barn back up to code after the fire would be costly and time-consuming. She hadn't even started looking at buying cattle and definitely didn't know the first thing about how to care for them. That bull had been larger than she'd expected up close. Were all cattle that big?

She also didn't like how he occasionally made sly, underhanded comments about her situation, her lack of experience, and the fact she was a city girl. Still, she chalked it up to him coming from a different generation where men didn't always treat women as equals. Not that this made it right for him to put her down, but it at least explained his behavior.

In the following days, Piper found Noah dropping by more and more often. He always seemed like he wanted to say something but was reluctant to give voice to whatever was bothering him. She tried several times to coax it out of him, but he always found a way to shrug it off.

"Oh, little miss, I almost forgot," he started, as he was leaving one evening, "a friend of mine who owes me a favor said he will meet with you to discuss selling some cattle to you."

Cattle? Her eyes went wide at the thought of them. "Thank you, but I'm not looking at buying any cattle just yet, I need to fix the barn first." She smiled back at him, hoping this would be the end of the matter, but he stood fast in the doorway.

He chuckled. "How do you expect to run a cattle ranch without any cattle?"

It felt like he was laughing at her. Piper fought to maintain her pleasant expression. She didn't like being mocked. She was starting to see a different side to Noah, as he grew more comfortable in her company, and liked less and less of what she saw. Different generations didn't begin to excuse the cutting comments or mocking look in his eye. Especially now as he spoke with such a condescending tone.

"Look, little miss, at least meet with him and know what your options are."

Options. She frowned. She needed cattle but dealing with someone whom Noah recommended didn't feel like a good idea. All the same, was there any harm in getting some information? She thought about it for a moment and agreed. At least then, she could work out her finances for fixing the barn and know how much she had left for cattle and of course, a horse or two.

Noah sent Job over the following day with the address and details of where and when to meet the cattle auctioneer. She showered, fed the ranch hands, and gave them a list of supplies to buy and jobs to start on.

They were still rebuilding the barn and had a long way to go. Somewhat dissatisfied to be wasting her day like this, she headed out.

She arrived at the cattle auction and instantly felt out of her depth. It was everything she'd been afraid it would be. The auction barn was crowded, loud, and the smell of manure was an insult to the senses. Everyone seemed to take the cattle auction so seriously, pushing past each other, screaming and hollering to be heard. She stood and watched a few rounds of bidding before she went to meet Noah's friend.

"Okay, folks, here it is, a young Hereford, weighing in at a beautiful five hundred and fifty pounds, isn't she a beaut? She's from a prize-winning line and is perfect for breeding. She isn't going to go cheap. Shall we start the bidding at fifteen hundred dollars? Do I hear sixteen hundred?" yelled the auctioneer into his megaphone. The crowd groaned, obviously not happy with the starting bid. Piper didn't know much about cattle. Still, she was glad to see she wasn't the only one concerned. "Surely that's not right," she said out loud.

A woman with short black hair overheard her comment, turned to her, and snarled, "Leave the buying to the professional's sweet cheeks. Why not go back to your dream house and cook a pie for your sugar daddy?" The woman ended her comment with a cackle as she pushed past Piper to the front of the crowd closest to the heifer.

Piper felt dizzy as, slowly, people started bidding. The bidding ended at over five thousand dollars. A proper herd would cost more than it would to rebuild her barn. She felt sick and decided her meeting was pointless, she pushed through the crowds to her truck and drove back home.

Twelve

JOB WAITED UNTIL NIGHTFALL. He drove the truck pulling a cattle trailer behind. He drove up to the barn to find Noah and Frank talking outside. "She's back boss," he chimed as he climbed out of the truck. He went to the back and opened the trailer leading the prize Hereford into the barn."

Did she come to see you?" Noah asked Frank, blowing his cigar smoke into the air

"No, your plan worked perfectly. I saw her in the crowd as soon as bidding got past fifteen hundred she left," he chuckled, stroking the cow as Job walked it past, his caress was met by a lowing sound from the young heifer.

"J, did she see you?" Noah asked, blowing smoke in his direction.

"No sir, I hid in the back," he replied. Job, Noah, and Frank had set the whole thing up.

The Hereford was a new purchase of Noah's. Thankfully, when he gave Piper the tour of his ranch, the cow hadn't arrived yet. Job was rather proud of himself for suggesting Frank fake auctioning off the heifer. The woman he'd hired to buy it at an unreasonable price hopefully scared Piper off. Job didn't want the Baker Ranch to succeed any more than Noah did. After all, when the Baker Ranch was at its peak, it often outperformed every other ranch in the county. If it became a success once more, Job wasn't sure his boss could compete, and that would mean the loss of the ranch and, in turn, his home and livelihood.

Job found himself offering his opinion a lot more of late, helping the already scheming mind of Noah Martinez. The next stage of their plan was already in place. Poor little miss Piper wouldn't know what hit her. She may have had everyone else in town fooled that she was all sweet and innocent, but Job didn't believe it for a second. He had seen enough in his fifty years to know that no one was that nice. Everyone had an agenda. Everyone was out for themselves, himself included. Even Noah's children wanted nothing to do with him or the ranch, and the last thing they heard, his wife had passed away not long after she left. It had been agreed that on Mr. Martinez's passing, the ranch would go to Job, his oldest employee and friend. If the ranch failed, he would lose everything he had worked all his life to help build. He was not about to let that happen.

Thirteen

PIPER WAS happy with her staff's progress in rebuilding the barn, although she couldn't help but think she would be much further along if Sawyer was still a part of the team. She sat at the dining table looking over all the paperwork and bank statements and sighed. "It would probably cost less if Sawyer were here too," she out loud, burying her face in her hands. She assumed the vendors were charging her more because she was a young, inexperienced woman who didn't know how to haggle. As it turned out, she was right. Looking over the receipts she had from when Sawyer was working for her, she noticed a drastic price increase in what she was now paying.

Great. Just great.

She spent several days traveling around town and even ventured to nearby towns to try and get a better deal. Still, each time she was met with the same response, "Supply and demand, ma'am, prices increase all the time. It's just business." Now, as she looked over her bank statements, she was starting to think she had bitten off more than she could chew. The increased cost of supplies was beginning to eat at her funds at an alarming rate. The settlement from her divorce lawyer would run out if she weren't more careful with spending. "If things carry on like this,

I'm not going to be able to pay the ranch hands," she said to herself. "How am I supposed to build this place alone?"

After an hour of trying to figure out where she could afford to cut back, she gave up and went to bed.

Things went from bad to worse over the following week. She woke up one morning to find a water pipe had burst next to the water trough in the corral. She stood looking over the waterlogged land trying not to let her ranch hands see how anxious she felt. The entire area was a muddy morass, unfit for horses or cattle. Just when she thought things couldn't get any worse, they did.

One morning she came down to find two more ranch hands had packed up and left. Then another morning, when she was making breakfast, she opened the cupboard under the sink to find a large diamondback rattlesnake. She screamed and slammed the door closed just before it had a chance to strike and bite her.

"Ma'am, is everything ok?" asked the youngest ranch hand.

"Snake. Under the sink," she panted.

"I'll call animal control," he informed her and left her alone. She sank to the floor and curled up, leaning against the fridge after piling everything that wasn't nailed down against the cabinet to make sure it didn't escape. "Man, I can't catch a break."

At the end of the week, Noah stopped by. Piper was out on the back porch watching the sunset when he arrived. She didn't hear him walk up behind her and jumped out of her seat when he greeted her hello.

"Jeeze, Noah. You scared the life out of me," she gasped, clutching her chest. Her heartbeat thundering hard against her palm.

He smiled and let out a small laugh. "Sorry, little miss."

"Please stop calling me that," she said, causing Noah to raise an eyebrow of surprise.

She debated how much of an issue she wanted to make of this. In the end, she decided it wasn't worth it. "I've told you, please call me Piper."

He nodded and sat in the chair next to her. "News on the vine is you had a flood and found a snake," he said, pulling out a cigar and lighting it, tossing the match to the floor.

Piper didn't like the smell of his cigar but didn't want to be rude. "How did you hear that?" she asked as she sat back down.

"News travels fast in these here parts." He pulled out a silver hip flask from his inside pocket and handed it to her. "Thought you might like a drink and a shoulder to cry on."

Piper was taken aback by his comment. She was anxious and stressed, but for him to assume she was emotionally unstable vexed her. "Thanks, but a lady cries in private," she said softly, not meeting his gaze as she took the flask from him. She opened it and was met with the woody fragrance of Noah's favorite whiskey. It was something she'd been coming to like. Her mouth watered for the alcohol. Her entire body craved it.

'*What would be the harm?*' she thought. She took a drink and passed it back.

"Didn't mean to offend, but so that you know, I have been told I'm a wonderful listener."

After a few sips, she sighed. She *did* want to talk to someone about her worries. They sat out on the porch until the early hours of the morning. Piper spilled her guts about everything from her finances, the staff leaving, the flood, and even felt comfortable enough to share the details of her divorce from John. Noah sat back, listening intently, saying nothing. When Piper finally stopped talking, she looked over to see a look of concern creasing Noah's face. She worried she had over-shared again, and he would leave her just like Sawyer had.

Being in the town alone away from all her family, she didn't want to lose another friend. "I'm sorry, I've said too much," she said looking off into the distance.

"Not at all, I'm glad you feel you can talk to me, it's just," he started, rubbing the back of his neck anxiously, but didn't finish the thought.

"It's just what?"

"I didn't want to say anything, but there are rumors that your ranch is cursed," he replied.

Piper burst out laughing. *Cursed*? He surely couldn't believe that, could he? She looked over and to her surprise, his face was stone serious. "I'm sorry, I didn't mean to laugh but you can't seriously believe that can you?" she asked.

Noah stared back at her for a few moments; his eyes were as cold and unblinking as that rattlesnake's had been. It unsettled Piper, causing her to shuffle in her chair.

"I'm not usually a suspicious man, Miss Piper. I believe what my eyes tell me, and I may not have believed it in the past, but given every-thing you have said, you can't deny there may be some truth in it all."

Piper sat thinking over his words, did he have a point? "Cursed how?" she asked humoring him, but also curious enough to want to hear the rest of the story.

Noah went on to tell her a tale that the ranch was rumored to be built on an old Indian burial ground and how every owner had been plagued with problems and financial difficulties. He told her that the previous owner died mysteriously, and because his death couldn't be explained, it was marked as natural causes. "The last owner's family tried to sell this place for years, but no one was interested because of its history. The place sat empty for decades. Now, with the fire, the flood, and that snake...well I don't know what to think. It's rare for a rattlesnake to enter a dwelling."

Not impressed with his reasoning, Piper shrugged off his comments, saying it was all a coincidence.

She politely excused herself off to bed, and Noah left. She lay in bed that night, staring at the ceiling and listening to the insects outside her window. Noah's words and the events of the last few weeks played out in front of her eyes.

What if he has a point?

She didn't sleep much that night.

Fourteen

SAWYER SAT on the end of his bed, flicking through the T.V. channels in the dingy motel he was staying at for the night. After leaving the ranch, he hadn't known where to go and found himself wandering highway after highway, staying at any motel he could find. He knew he needed to plan. He couldn't carry on like this. Without a job, money would run out fast.

That wasn't the only thing that concerned him. Piper hadn't left his thoughts since the night he left, and he felt awful for ditching her after her breakdown at dinner. She had tried to contact him several times since his departure, but he'd ignored each one of her calls, not knowing how to explain why he left so abruptly. What must she think of him? But he couldn't afford to stay; it was too dangerous.

The threatening notes had started about a month after he moved onto the ranch. They were nothing at first. Things like *'leave'* and *'Go home or else.'* He ignored the letters at first, thinking it was a prank, or maybe even one of the ranch hands trying to scare him off so they could take his job.

Then the notes became more threatening. *'If you don't leave, I will kill you. You're a dead man if you stay at the ranch.'* Maybe he should have contacted the authorities. Especially when the last note came. Instead, he left. He still had the note in his pocket.

If I don't leave, they'll kill her too.

It had seemed cowardly to go. But what made matters worse was during the night before he left, he heard footsteps outside his door. When he got up to check, he saw the shadow under the door and heard the tell-tale click of the hammer being pulled back on a revolver. Revolvers were a popular gun of choice in these parts, and he had seen the damage done by them up close and personal. Close enough to be scared now.

Until that night, he didn't take the notes seriously. But when he heard someone with a gun outside his room, it dawned on him that these threats could be real. He liked Piper and had grown fond of their friendship, but he didn't want to risk his life for a woman he barely knew. Certainly not for a steady income.

He remembered Peggy lying on the kitchen floor. The memory was clear as day in his mind. When he heard the gun's cylinder spinning, the body on the floor in his mind changed to Piper. He couldn't save Peggy, but if leaving guaranteed Piper's safety as well as his own, that's exactly what he planned to do.

I should have called the authorities. At least anonymously or something.

But he hadn't. What proof did he have without giving them the notes? The problem was the moment that he would have brought them to the cop's attention they would have looked right square at him. He couldn't afford to be under that kind of scrutiny. Not again.

So, he'd run. He packed everything and left that very night. Every night since, he found his mind drifting back to Piper. How was she? Was she still in danger? Had he managed to save her? And maybe he had no right to wonder if, but did she miss him? Over the short time with Piper, he had grown quite fond of her. She was a good friend, a good boss, and a good woman.

He felt his mind spiraling down a dark path he had struggled to drag himself out of. "Pull yourself together, man." He spoke to his empty room.

Eventually, he decided it was time for bed, but sleep didn't come easy. His mind still wanted to do battle. He tossed and turned, sweating profusely in his sleep with bloody images dancing in his mind.

Piper was running around the ranch crying, screaming his name. She was hurt but he didn't know how. She was bleeding but her wound was unclear. He heard footsteps but everywhere he looked was empty, who was there?

He followed Piper around the ranch trying to get her attention, but she couldn't see him, he tried to reach out to her, but she was always just a touch out of reach.

"No, please don't" she sobbed, as a faceless shadow raised a revolver in her direction. A single shot rang in his ears, the bullet didn't hit Piper, but she disappeared in a cloud of smoke and the faceless shadow walked away.

"Who are you?" he screamed, chasing after it. "Come back here and answer me!"

It entered the barn closing the door behind it. Sawyer followed but when he flung open the door he froze in place. A face he didn't expect to see stared back at him. A lump in his throat choked him, and tears stung his eyes. "Peg?" He couldn't breathe.

"You left her? After what happened to me?" Tears brimmed in her eyes. "Go back for her. She isn't safe."

He reached out to his late wife, but before he could touch her, she too vanished in a puff of smoke.

He woke screaming and gasping for breath. The dream felt too real. He sat up, shivering, cold sweat drying on his skin. It was no use trying to sleep further. He went into the bathroom and splashed cold water on his face. His reflection showed a haggard man with haunted eyes. He made a decision. "Tomorrow morning, I'm going back."

Fifteen

PIPER DECIDED she needed a change of scenery from her farmhouse, so she opted to have breakfast at the diner. She needed to be around other people and away from the ranch for a while. She liked the food at the diner, eggs Benedict being her favorite. After a satisfying breakfast and cappuccino, she headed to the hardware store to stock up on a few supplies before she drove back home.

It was a beautiful day with a cool breeze that caressed her skin, a nice change from the hot humid days they'd been having. Not quite ready to return just yet, she drove the long way home so she could admire the town, something she wanted to do a lot more of now that this place was home.

"Seriously, you again?" she said to herself as she pulled up to her farmhouse to find Noah sitting on the porch waiting for her. While she appreciated her neighbor worrying about her, his energetic visits were starting to drag her down. More and more she wanted to tell him to just go away.

"Hello again, Noah." She smiled, trying her hardest not to let her frustrations play out on her face.

"Miss Piper, I have been thinking about you and your current unfortunate circumstances," he said by way of greeting. "I have a business proposition for you. Is now a good time to talk?" He crushed his cigar under his boot on her freshly laid pathway.

Piper looked down at the mess in alarm. She couldn't understand why he thought this was an OK thing to do. She would never treat someone else's property with such disregard or disrespect. "You are here aren't you?" she asked, struggling to school her features to something neutral. "Now is as good a time as any. Come in. Do you want a coffee?" She led the way through the house to the kitchen.

Noah settled at the kitchen table, surveying his surroundings like he owned the place. It was plain to see he didn't agree with some of her decorating choices, especially the way he turned his nose up at the napkin holder on the table she'd just recently bought from a little antique store just off the highway. "You know, I think I will thank you, little miss. Er...I mean *Piper*. Cream, four sugars, please." He slammed a small leather satchel-style briefcase on the table, Piper hadn't even noticed him carrying it in. The sudden bang made Piper jump and almost spill her coffee all over herself.

This seemed to amuse Noah. He laughed. "You scare too easy, little miss. Shall we begin?"

Piper noted, not for the first time, how he seemed to find enjoyment in her discomfort. It angered her, but she was too polite to say anything. "Sure." She spoke through gritted teeth. Whatever he wanted, she hoped it wouldn't take long.

By the time Noah had finished presenting Piper with his proposition, she felt the weight of the world settling on her shoulders. He had presented her with facts and figures. She couldn't argue with what was in black and white on the page in front of her. Repairs, expenses, permits, licenses, memberships, and a lot of other things she hadn't even considered were lined up in neat columns with numbers attached. He reiterated her concerns and worries but coming from someone else's lips made them feel even more severe. Without thinking, she asked, "What am I going to do?"

She was asking herself, not Noah, but he grinned all the same and answered, "I'm so glad you asked that particular question." He pulled a brown envelope from his bag and slid it across the table to Piper.

"Think it over, and when you feel ready, head over to my place, and we can get the paperwork signed." He smiled, saluting with his freshly lit cigar as he left the kitchen through the side door and headed toward his car.

Piper had no words. When he'd handed her the papers and suggested she sell to him, she had fallen silent. For the first time in a long time, she felt empty and lost. This ranch was her chance at independence, a chance to make a life of her own. How could it all be over so quickly?

She sat in bed that night looking over everything he had left her, and she couldn't lie to herself. The offer was tempting. She didn't want to believe that she had lasted less than 6 months on her own. Yet, if she sold, she would have a nice sum of money to start a new life somewhere else. But what was she supposed to do? Wander the world aimlessly and spend the nest egg he was offering her? No, she supposed she would have to head home to her parents with her tail between her legs. Only admitting that mom was right wasn't an option. She'd rather die than go back.

"Why does he want my ranch anyway? Why would he even want it if there's so much wrong with it? I mean, if it's a drain on finances, and even *cursed*," his lip curled at the word, "why would he want the place?" The rational side of her brain was waking up. None of this made sense. She looked over the papers one last time before she tossed them in a drawer and headed to bed.

Selling Baker Ranch would have to be tomorrow's problem.

Sixteen

SAWYER BATTLED with how to approach the situation. He didn't want to alarm Piper by telling her that he'd heard someone with a gun outside his room or about the threatening notes. He had no idea how to explain why he had up and left without a word. He imagined she would be angry with him, and he worried about whether she would even allow him back on the ranch. But what bothered him most was that he still had no idea who sent the notes or if they intended to act on their threats.

As he drove past the town sign welcoming him back, he decided to head to a bar on the other side of town just to make sure he wouldn't accidentally bump into Piper. He didn't want to see her just yet. He wanted to get his story straight.

The bar he chose was one frequented by ranch hands. Like many such cowboy bars, it had a mechanical bull in the back where guys whooped and hollered as they showed off for their female counterparts. There was a singular pool table that was so old and in disrepair, it had a wedge of wood under one leg to stop it from tipping. The green felt surface was worn in several places, giving the players extra obstacles to work around. Behind them, a dartboard was surrounded by puncture marks in the wall from missed shots.

Sawyer sat at the far end of the bar, tucked in the corner away from the crowds, but with a good view of the room so he could watch everyone go about their business. "What are you having?" asked the bartender, a young red-headed woman dressed in jeans and an overly tight white t-shirt. It was very low-cut and highlighted her cleavage. She wore a straw cowboy hat to match the theme of the bar.

"Just a beer, thanks," he said pulling out his wallet and handing her a bill.

"Your change," she replied sliding the bottle across to him, along with a handful of ones.

He sat slowly drinking his beer trying to think of what to say to Piper, wondering if he was making the right decision, coming back.

"Nah, man it's hard out here. I can't find a job anywhere," a voice behind him complained.

"What about that old ranch that sweet young thing is trying to fix up? I'm sure she is going to need extra help. I heard her ranch manager up and left. Since that barn fire, she can't keep hands on the place," came a reply.

Sawyer sat up slightly turning his head in the direction of the conversation. His heart rate quickened at the thought of a fire at the ranch. *Was she hurt? Who left? How did the fire start?* He had too many questions and not enough answers.

"Nah man, I heard bad things about that ranch" the first voice replied, Sawyer turned around to see who was talking.

At the table just behind him sat old man Peters and his son-in-law, Patrick.

"What kind of things?" Sawyer asked ignoring the annoyed glance he received. They clearly didn't like a stranger butting into their conversation.

"Someone has been going around town warning off all farm and ranch hands, saying it's dangerous to be involved with her and that ranch."

"I'm going to need clarification here, cowboy," Sawyer said, taking his beer to join them at the table, ignoring their looks of confusion.

"Sorry bud, but do we know you?" Patrick asked.

"Not personally, but I know who you guys are. I've seen you around town," he replied, turning his back on the young man to focus all his attention on the old guy who seemed to have all the answers.

"So, you were saying, a fire? What happened?"

Old man Peters was all too keen to answer. He was known for being as much of a gossip as some of the women in town. "No one knows. All I heard was the barn caught fire early hours of the morning and burned most of the way down through the night. They struggled to put it out, took them a good few hours to stop it from spreading across the ranch. Apparently, the owner was nowhere to be found and no one knew if they should call the fire department or not. Fools. Every last one of them."

Sawyer sat back and drank off the remainder of his beer. *'There was nothing in the barn that could easily cause a fire,'* he thought to himself. "Do they suspect arson?" he asked, his mind shifting back to the threatening notes.

"No clue. Why, do you think they should be? I mean, it would make sense, with everyone being warned not to take work on the ranch."

"Warned by who?" Sawyer demanded.

"Don't know, some out of towner. Never saw him before. Tall guy, pretty serious looking. Dark hair I think. He paid people pretty handsomely to avoid helping the poor girl," old man Peters replied with a shrug.

"Anything else?" Sawyer asked.

"Nothing serious. There was a flooded corral, pipe burst I think. I also heard they called in animal control. Some rattlesnake infestation or something."

At that, Sawyer got up and left.

Seventeen

PIPER JUMPED, startled by the hammering on the front door. It was almost ten-thirty. "Who could that be?" she asked the empty room as she cautiously headed for the door.

"Piper," came Sawyer's voice from behind the door.

Piper felt a rush of emotion, mixed feelings of anger, followed by relief at his return. "Sawyer?" she asked fiddling with the multiple locks. She swung the door open and Sawyer pushed right past her. "What the hell, Sawyer?" she protested, as she stumbled back to give him room.

"What's going on? I've heard there was a fire, a flood, and something about a rattlesnake infestation?"

"Where did you hear all that?" she asked, following him back into the living room.

He paced the space like a caged animal, it unsettled Piper. "News travels fast around here."

"So, I've heard," she muttered sourly. "What do you care? You left without so much as a word." All her anger, frustration, and anxiety from the last few weeks churned inside of her. She felt like a volcano about to explode, and poor Sawyer was going to be her next victim.

"Look, I'm sorry, I had something I needed to take care of," he said rubbing the back of his neck.

"So what? Do you think you can just come back like nothing happened? I was worried sick. I thought something terrible had happened to you! I searched hospitals, fields, everywhere, only to find you packed up your stuff and ran. Was I not a good employer? I thought we had respect for each other, clearly, I was wrong." She pointed toward the door. "I really don't need this right now. I suggest you leave."

"Look, we can either go round and round in circles, or you can tell me what's happened here," he said, standing firmly in front of her. They stared at each other for a while before Piper let out the breath she was holding and slammed the door, then slumped down on the nearby sofa.

Figuring she had no one else to tell about all the crazy things that had been happening to her, she proceeded to regale him with the week's events and Noah's crazy notion that the ranch was cursed.

"Why didn't you call me after the fire?" he asked, slumping down beside her, one hand rubbing his face roughly.

Piper chuckled. She knew how he felt. "And say what? Oh hi, former employee who went AWOL, I recently had a fire, care to come help?" Her tone didn't hide the bitterness she felt. "What does it even matter? Maybe Noah was right, and I'd be better off selling to someone who knows what they're doing,"

Sawyer suddenly sat bolt upright. "Come again?" he asked.

Piper gave him a look and went over the sideboard to pull out the paperwork, handing it to him silently.

"Sell to who?" Sawyer asked, thumbing through the documents.

"Noah Martinez."

She told him about her conversation with Noah the previous evening and how, after a lot of thought, she was considering his offer. It felt good talking to Sawyer. Even though she was still mad at him for abandoning the ranch the way he did, she was glad he was back.

"Please tell me you don't believe this crap?" he asked, tossing the papers onto the coffee table.

"It's not even that. What drives me crazy is he's right. I haven't a clue what I'm doing, I don't belong here, and this past week proves it. Maybe I should sell out, move home and start my life somewhere new."

Sawyer's next question threw Piper. "Why did you come here in the first place?"

Piper sighed and retold her story without the influence of alcohol this time. She couldn't bring herself to look at Sawyer when she told it. She just kept her eyes on the frayed corner of the blanket she had wrapped around herself. The longer she talked, the more she felt an invisible weight lifting from her shoulders. Even as tears welled in her eyes, she recognized this time her reason for crying was different. She was no longer full of pain like she was when John came home to tell her he had got his side piece pregnant and left her after ten years together. These were tears of relief.

She had been bottling everything up inside her for too long. She hadn't even told her parents the entire story, too afraid of how they would react. Talking to Sawyer was different though. He'd been interested as she talked, asking questions that proved he was listening. Even now his expression was sympathetic. "Do you know how brave you are?" he asked simply.

Not expecting that to be his first response, she sat up, cocking her head to one side to look at him. "Excuse me?" she asked.

His expression was serious, though his eyes burned with something more. Admiration? "You left everything you had ever known, to start a new life on your own. What's more, you're doing it on your terms. You are *finally* doing something for yourself. Do you understand the strength it takes to do something like that?"

Piper wiped the tears from her face and smiled weakly back at him. "I never looked at it that way before." A warmth spread through her chest at his words, and she found she was looking at him through different eyes. It was as though she was seeing Sawyer for the first time. She liked what she saw.

He walked across the room and crouched down in front of her, resting his hands on her knees. His touch, even through the blanket, sent a jolt of electricity through Piper. She stared in surprise. She couldn't explain her reaction. In truth, she didn't want to.

"Are you going to give all this up?" Sawyer gestured with a broad sweep of his arm taking in the room, the house, the entire ranch in a single movement. "Everything you have worked for, everything you have dreamed of. Just because of a few setbacks, and the crazy words from some lying buffoon only out for himself?" Sawyer asked softly, staring deeply into Piper's eyes.

She considered these words, turning them over in her mind. He was right. She was never more sure of anything in her life.

The next morning Piper found Sawyer back at her front door. "So, do I get my job back or are you still selling?" he asked, with a slight smile.

"I haven't sold the ranch yet, so you may as well take your job back until I figure out what I'm going to do." She smiled back, inviting him in and helping him carry his things back to his old room.

"Piper, please tell me you are not still considering it?" he asked. She noticed how, yet again, he called her Piper. Before he left, she had insisted he call her Piper, but he always stuck to the formal 'ma'am.' She liked how her name sounded coming from his mouth.

All the same, she sighed deeply, folding her arms, and leaning against his door. "No. You were right. I can't let a few setbacks and someone else's superstitions get in my way. This is my ranch, and I'm going to keep it. Though I'll admit, it's not going to be easy getting this place back on its feet."

He smiled. "It's a good thing the best ranch manager in town is on the payroll then isn't it, ma'am?" he said, adding a wink so over the top she couldn't help but give a wistful smile, for she felt a bit hurt that 'Piper' was gone and somehow 'ma'am' had made a comeback.

Eighteen

A WEEK HAD PASSED since Noah made his offer to buy the ranch from Piper, and he hadn't heard a word from her. He paced the small room just off the living room that he had turned into his office. He also noticed she had started to rebuild the barn. He couldn't figure out how, since he had paid everyone he could think of quite handsomely to make sure the supplies she needed would be unaffordable to her. Last he heard, she had lost a few ranch hands as well, so how she was pulling this off alone, he couldn't understand. He wanted that land. He needed it.

Noah had sent Job to check out the property a few times, and each time he returned with no information. The fences and front gate had been secured, and he couldn't get in. Noah hated it when things didn't go according to his plans. "Why hasn't she signed the papers yet?"

He whipped the glass in his hand across the room, shattering it against the wall next to the antique grandfather clock, another item he owned that had been passed down from his father. Noah had a reputation for having a bad temper, but over the years, he had gotten better at controlling it. Or masking it, at least. He stared at the stain of alcohol on the wall, the whiskey trickling down the paneling. He could feel his temperature rising, his blood began to boil as if the stain there was her fault too. The longer she waited to sign, the more chance she had to change her mind. He was so sure he had convinced her to sell that night. She tried to hide it, but he could see she believed every lie he told her.

A knock came at his door and Job walked in.

"What?" Noah yelled, his face tight and red with anger.

Job came and sat at the chair in front of the large mahogany desk. "You're not going to like this boss," he started.

Noah stood watching impatiently, waiting for him to continue. "Well? Spit it out already," he yelled.

Job didn't even flinch. He'd seen enough of Noah's outbursts to know he was all talk. "Word is that ranch manager is back in town."

Noah slammed his hand down hard on the desk. "What? I thought we got rid of him! You told me he left!" he yelled, leaning over the desk towards Job, who still sat unbothered by the anger thrown in his direction.

"He did. And now he's back. Old man Peters saw him in that cowboy bar across town," Job told him. "Said he was asking a lot of questions."

Noah sat down in his oversized Chesterfield leather chair. "What kind of questions?" he asked.

Job shrugged.

"Then what the hell am I paying you for? I would be better getting my information from old man Peters, the town gossip," Noah roared back at him.

Job never so much as flinched. "All I know is Peters' son-in-law was complaining about the lack of work and when Peters started talking about the fire, this guy came and butted in, asking all kinds of questions. Next thing he knew, the guy up and left."

Noah finally had his answer. If the ranch manager was back in town *that's* why the rebuilding had begun. '*If she's shown him that paperwork, he'll know it's a load of trash*' he thought. "Is he back on the ranch?" Noah asked, grabbing a fresh glass from the sideboard and pouring himself a whiskey from the nearest bottle. He poured one for Job and slid it over to him.

"I don't know. Last I heard, he was back in town but was staying in

Gina's motel. Hopefully, that bitch sent him packing again," Job replied after a slow sip.

Noah pondered this. "You could be right. From all the yammering she did, I could tell she wouldn't take kindly to a man walking out on her again, not after that ex of hers dropped the divorce bombshell on her and left."

♡

After another two days with no word from Piper, Noah's patience had run out. "Job! Get your no-good ass in here," he yelled through his office door.

"Boss?" Job asked, popping his head around the door frame.

"Has our little city slicker been in touch?"

Job shook his head.

"Any more news on our ranch manager problem?" Noah asked, getting increasingly agitated with every shake of Job's head.

"No boss," he replied and ran out the door as Noah picked up the large brass bull-shaped paperweight off the table and lobbed it at the door. He missed the frame and hit the wall in the hallway, making a hole in the drywall. "Useless, everyone around here is useless! Why do I waste my money on you? If I want something done right, I have to do it myself," he yelled. He needed the papers signed, and he needed them signed now. He wasn't prepared to wait for a second longer. Grabbing his pocket-size cigar case, a box of matches, and car keys, he decided he was going over to talk to his little city problem himself. He only paused long enough to grab something from the safe hidden behind a painting of his ranch on his way out.

He arrived at the ranch to find the gates securely locked. There was a small gate just next to it, just big enough for someone to pass through on foot. Forced to leave his car, he groaned in frustration. He slammed his door, lit a cigar, and barged through the gate. Storming up the property towards the ranch house, he saw a car he thought he had seen before, parked by the outbuildings. He paused to study it, realizing he needed to calm down before he spoke to little miss Piper. If he approached the subject of selling in his current state, she would surely back out.

Whoever had left the car didn't seem to be around. Putting on his most convincing smile, he strode the rest of the way up the driveway and knocked lightly on the door. A few moments passed, and no one answered. Glancing at the window, he could see the lights switched on inside, so he knew she had to be home. He knocked a little louder but still got no response. Anger rushed his veins once more. He walked around the side of the house, hoping to find someone outside working by the barn or someone who could tell him where their employer was. To his surprise, he found Piper and the ranch manager, whose name he never could remember, sharing a beer and talking on the back porch. They were so busy making googly eyes at each other, they hadn't noticed his approach. With a grunt of satisfaction, Noah slid into the shadows between the trees planted next to the porch and craned his neck so he could watch and hopefully listen to their conversation.

Nineteen

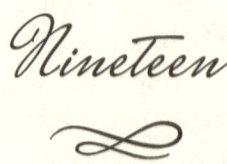

"THANK YOU," Piper said, smiling, taking in a deep breath. The smell of freshly cut wood, grass, and wildflowers filled her nose. The faint scent of manure traveled on the wind, but she had become adjusted to the smell of a ranch and now found it quite comforting.

"Just doing my job, ma'am," Sawyer replied, tilting his beer in salute.

Sawyer had been good for her, she realized. He'd made her open her eyes and revaluate everything. Since he'd come back, she gained an entirely new perspective on things, and looked forward to what the future could hold with more excitement than she'd ever previously had.

"No, I mean thank you for convincing me not to sell. You were right. I'd regret it years down the line if I gave up so soon." She smiled. Maybe things weren't perfect, but this ranch was hers and she intended on making it the biggest and best ranch in the county.

"It's my pleasure, ma'am."

"Will you please call me Piper?" she insisted with a chuckle.

"Oh, I almost forgot, I got the reports back about the pipe that burst in the corral," Sawyer said, reaching into his back pocket and pulling out a sheet of paper, which he handed to her.

Piper didn't understand what she was reading, and she looked over to Sawyer, mystified. "I don't understand any of this." She laughed and shook her head. "It says the pipe didn't burst. That an impact fracture caused the break?"

"You've got the right of it," Sawyer said. "That's exactly what happened."

Piper let his words sink in for a moment. Impact fracture? "Are you saying it was done on purpose? Like someone tried to break the pipe?" she asked, not wanting an answer because deep down, she already knew.

If this was done intentionally, the problems that she thought she had put behind her were about to get a whole lot bigger.

Sawyer nodded, taking a sip of his beer as though he needed time to think about what he was going to say before he said it. "While we're at it, it makes me think the fire was started intentionally too," he said finally.

Piper sat up, alarmed. "No. Why would someone *do* that? *Who* would *do* that?" she asked, her mind trying to piece everything together. Sawyer sat silently, allowing her to reach the same conclusion he already had. "No! Sawyer, you don't think all this was done to try and scare me out of town?" she asked finally.

Sawyer shook his head slowly. "Not to scare you, ma'am, but maybe it was to convince you that you couldn't do this alone. I'm thinking someone wants to give you enough financial strain and heartache to want to sell out. Probably for some ridiculously low price."

Everything that happened next felt like a blur. Time seemed to speed up and go in slow motion all at once. A creak in the porch floorboard from behind Piper caught her attention first. She glanced over her shoulder in time to see a shadow moving around the corner. "Who's there?" she asked.

Sawyer leaped to his feet. "Stay put!"

The next thing she knew, Noah burst out of the shadows, all red-faced and sweating. He was yelling some nonsense or another, the words jumbling together in his fury. "You couldn't leave well enough alone, could you? Interfering in other people's business!"

Piper thought he was talking to her until she saw where he was looking and realized he was pointing his rage at Sawyer. "You have to be the stupidest man I have ever met; someone makes a threat and what do you do? Run right back! I had this little bitch right where I wanted her, and you came along and ruined all my plans."

Piper didn't like being talked about that way. She pushed past Sawyer, who attempted to grab her and yank her back. Piper had had her fill with being told what to do, and now that she had decided to keep the ranch, she didn't like the idea of someone trespassing, nor was she in any mood to have someone else fight her battles. "Who the hell do you think you are talking to? Get the hell off my property before I call the police and have you arrested for trespassing," she yelled, already reaching for her phone.

"I'll teach you to interfere with my business. You mess with my life, I'll end yours!" Noah screamed charging towards them. He reached into his back pocket and pulled out a handgun with a long muzzle. Piper had never been a fan of guns and didn't know much about them, but she knew enough to take cover when she saw one. Or at least she thought she did. Her breath caught in her throat and her entire body became stiff as she froze in fear. She had never had a gun pulled on her before and couldn't seem to make herself move. Sawyer grabbed her arm and pulled her back, spinning her around, so he had his back to Noah, acting as a human shield as he tried to follow her down, away from the obvious threat.

There was a loud bang that echoed across the ranch. A flash of light she barely saw over Sawyer's shoulder. Sawyer had pushed Piper to the floor, and she hit hard, screaming. Above her, she saw Sawyer's face twist in pain. He had been shot.

Her heart thundered until surely it would burst from her chest. Her head felt strange, like she was seeing things from a long way away. This couldn't be happening. None of this could be happening.

"No! Help! Help! Somebody, please help!" she screamed at the top of her lungs. Sawyer hit the ground and was still.

Twenty

SAWYER FELL SO FAST that Piper would never, ever forget it. Just as she'd always remember the startled, pained look on his face just before he crumpled to the ground. After that, everything seemed to move in strange, slow, jagged motions. As if they were battery-operated movements, quickly losing their juice. Strangely though, her frantic screams retained their full power, piercing the peaceful afternoon like a shrieking, wounded bird taking flight.

She soon heard multiple running footsteps, racing through the grass from the barn and leaping onto the porch.

"What happened?! Ms. Baker, are you OK? Sawyer!"

Tim, her ranch hand, grimaced with concern. He and Will, another helper, gently shook Sawyer. To Piper's tremendous relief, he grunted and opened his eyes.

"Sawyer, oh my God, Sawyer, can you hear me?" Piper cried.

He looked up at her in strained, unwelcome confusion, but he clearly heard her every word.

"He's been shot," Piper gasped, looking at Tim and Will in desperation. "Did you see Noah Martinez drive off?"

"Noah? No..." Will was dumbfounded.

Tim also shook his head, as he helped Sawyer sit up. Piper immediately gasped, stifling her scream as blood pulsed from Sawyer's right temple, flowing freely down to his cheek. She'd somehow not noticed the wound in her own stunned confusion. My God, she thought, he's been shot in the head!

"Take a deep breath, buddy. We're going to help you stand up," Tim said.

"No!" Piper's shriek stunned the men. "I'm going to call an ambulance. Keep him still. There's no telling how close the bullet is to his brain."

"Ma'am..." Tim's voice was gentle.

Lifting Sawyer's left arm for her to take a look, he smiled. "The bullet grazed him above the elbow. His head's bleeding, my guess is, from a good bump and scrape when he fell down."

"Oh," she suddenly felt stupid and silly, like a hysterical helpless child for overreacting, but realized she didn't care in the least.

Sawyer wasn't dead, that's all that mattered until they sorted things out. Groaning, but smiling, as his friends helped him hobble into the farmhouse to take a seat on the couch in the living room, Sawyer did his best to lighten the grim mood. For my benefit, Piper thought wryly. She did her best to keep her raging emotions and spiraling thoughts in check.

"Make sure you press down on that firmly," she instructed Sawyer a few minutes later, after Tim and Will had left. He held the fresh hand towel to his head.

It would *maybe* help stop the bleeding, at least if he didn't need stitches. But, judging by how quickly this second towel soaked through with blood, she guessed that wouldn't be the case. Strangely, his arm barely bled at all, despite there being a large raw spot where the bullet had brushed against his skin. Taking a deep breath, hoping to stop her shaking and steady her voice, she brought up the hospital once again.

"I'll be fine, don't you worry," Sawyer's smile was buoyant despite his obvious pain.

Suddenly his lax and casual attitude to his injuries and their alarming situation infuriated her. Why did men have to be so difficult? For all they knew, they were both still in grave danger. Martinez had been out of his mind with fury, and if he didn't calm down, he'd surely be back. Which gave her another perfect reason for suggesting they go into town right away.

"After I drop you off at the hospital, and I'm sure you don't have a concussion, I'm going straight to Sheriff Garcia's office to report that brutal, violent man."

Sawyer sighed. There was no way Piper would just drop this and simply let things rest until they figured out exactly what they were going to do. He knew better than to keep arguing with her. He'd learned a long time ago, that in any sort of disagreement with a woman, it was much simpler and easier to just acquiesce and acknowledge that she was right. And Piper was more headstrong and stubborn than most. He groaned loudly as he attempted to stand.

The room tilted and leaned as his dizziness took greater hold. Queasy and off-balance, he toppled back down into his seat. Blinking to clear his double vision, he saw two Pipers rushing towards him and grab his arm. After ensuring he was seated comfortably, she ran to get Tim and Will to garner their aid. Even with their assistance, he had trouble walking a straight line to Piper's truck.

"You look like you have one hell of a headache," she told him, as she took her eyes off the road for a second to watch him readjust the towel still pressed to his head.

"Yes, ma'am. That's one thing I sure won't argue about."

His persistent smile was infectious, and she finally gave in and smiled back. Hell, their situation was desperate and serious, but the least they could do was attempt to find some humor in it, lighten the mood somehow and take it in stride. Even so, she hoped the Sheriff would take what happened very seriously. The way things were going in this small town, Piper couldn't be sure of anything anymore.

Fighting her urge to just remain quiet and let Sawyer rest as she drove, she finally asked him about Juan Garcia, how long he'd been in office and what he was like. Within seconds, she wished she hadn't asked. The Sheriff was abrupt, opinionated, and belligerent. He didn't take kindly to women who knew their rights and demanded respect. In fact, he wasn't very successful at hiding his self-perceived superiority over women and animosity towards them at all. Ugh. Yet another obstacle to her security and safety. When would it end?

Before she had much of a chance to question Sawyer further, she saw Tri-County Regional Hospital's huge sign up ahead. She'd seen the building before off at a distance but never up close. For a second, she wondered why on earth they'd made their roadside sign so large. Towering so conspicuously near the medical buildings, it merely drew attention to the accompanying hospital's small size. It wasn't like someone would inadvertently zip past the buildings without the huge sign. Counties and towns around here were so small that everyone knew where absolutely everything was.

Stop being critical, she told herself chidingly. Just be glad there's a hospital in town at all. She pulled in to the first of only two entrances and wound around the small roadway within the parking lot to the Emergency doors.

"Stay here," she told Sawyer. "I don't want you to get dizzy and fall. I'll get help."

Sawyer suddenly felt incredibly guilty watching Piper stride through the automatic opening doors. If he hadn't come back, if he hadn't discouraged her from selling Baker Ranch, Martinez wouldn't have shown up with a gun. And if I hadn't jumped in front of her, he shuddered. She just might have taken the shot. Except it's mainly me Martinez is angry at, he reminded himself, for throwing a wrench in his well-laid plans. But he'll take it out on both Piper and me. He shifted in his seat. Unless we come up with a plan.

"Sawyer? Let us help you into the wheelchair," the middle-aged nurse smiled.

Flanked by two attendants, she managed to get him deposited into the wheelchair in one piece. As they wheeled him away, Piper called after him.

"Do *not* just tell them you feel fine!"

Twenty-One

KEEP YOUR COOL, she coached herself as she drove across town. Explain everything that's happened, including your suspicions about who's behind the fire that destroyed your barn. The hospital will provide medical records of Sawyer's injuries to substantiate Noah's attack. If only Will or Tim had seen Noah run away and drive off!

She was vacillating about whether to tell Sheriff Garcia about the threatening notes Sawyer had received as she pulled into the police building's parking lot. No, she decided quickly. Surely, Garcia will interview Sawyer about the shooting, and Sawyer can explain everything himself. It might be better coming from a man anyway, she sneered, remembering what she'd been told about Garcia's attitude as she opened the building's heavy front door.

Shocked for a second when she stepped inside, she paused uneasily and looked around. The main room was airy but much smaller than she'd expected. Three desks that she surmised were for the deputies sat empty at the moment. The room's lone occupant, a chubby red-haired, middle-aged woman, sat typing behind a smaller desk a few feet in front of a large wooden door. Sheriff Juan R. Garcia, the door's plaque read. Piper assumed the woman was his secretary.

Her footfalls echoed unnervingly as Piper strode towards her. She looked up, irritated, from the depths of her work.

"Yes?" her tone was curt and unfriendly, in contrast to her cheery nameplate with the smiley face glued on.

Piper knew better than to call her Madge.

"Hello Ms. Sterling, I have to see Sheriff Garcia right away. My employee and I have been attacked. He's been shot and is in Emergency at the hospital."

"Shot? I see..."

Madge's keen narrowed eyes bored right through her. Her unyielding expression was one of disbelief. Well, of course, Piper gathered her senses quickly. Cassidy Falls, population 11,103. Attempted murders were undoubtedly few and far between. The enduring silence painfully glued her and Madge together before Piper jumped in, deciding the secretary's quick retort was all she was going to get.

"Yes, shot. I'd like Sheriff Garcia to take a report."

"Would you, now..." Madge's tone was condescending.

How dare she demand what the Sheriff do.

"Is he in?" Piper's voice rose at least an octave.

Ditch polite, screw controlled, she seethed.

"Normally, the deputies take statements and make reports." They both turned their heads to stare at the empty desks. "They are all unavailable at the moment, so I'm afraid you will have to come back."

"Come back?!" Piper's response bordered on a scream. "Perhaps you didn't hear me correctly. My ranch hand's been shot, and I've just taken him to Emergency. Our attacker may very well be waiting for us when we get home."

Madge leaned back in her chair and glared up at her.

"You're welcome to wait. However, I'm not sure any of the deputies will return to the office before the end of their shift."

What?

"Can you page them? Is the Sheriff here?"

Within seconds they were arguing, batting words back and forth better than the best of the best on any debate team. Piper's heart jumped, and she gasped when Sheriff Garcia's door flew open.

"It's all right, Madge. Miss, step in."

Piper did her best to conceal her shaking as she walked by him. She wasn't sure what upset her the most, his secretary's condescending, lackadaisical attitude, or his intimidating demeanor. Either way, Piper sensed she was screwed. Pulling his chair away from his desk angrily, Garcia gestured for her to take the seat across from him. He threw his pastrami sandwich back into its Styrofoam container as she settled in place. Another brisk wave of his hand encouraged her to begin.

"Thank you, Sheriff. My name is Piper Baker, and I'm the new owner of...."

"Baker Ranch," he finished her sentence. "Yes, I know. We're a small town, and I know everything."

Put off for a second, she stammered and continued, painstakingly bringing Garcia up to date on everything. The fire, the purposely damaged pipe in the corral, Martinez's attack on her and Sawyer just a few hours ago. And, despite her initial resolve to not mention them, even the threats Sawyer had received.

"But, I'm sure you'll wish to have Sawyer explain about the notes when you take his statement and interview him."

"Other than you and your employee, did anyone else see what happened today?"

"No, I'm afraid not. The other ranch hands were busy at the barn. The two that came running to help following the shot, unfortunately, didn't see Noah Martinez leave."

"So," the Sheriff leaned back in his leather chair. "What this boils down to is your word, and your employee's word, against Martinez's."

"Sawyer has a gunshot wound!"

"But, other than you, no witness to events and to who held the gun."

Stunned, it took Piper a few seconds to realize her mouth was actually hanging open. She'd sighed deeply, opened her mouth to debate but had nothing to say. At least nothing she could think of that would sway the already decided mind of the biased Sheriff. *And it's not just because I'm a woman* was the infuriating thought that crept in. There's more going on here in Cassidy Falls than meets the eye, she reluctantly surmised. Finding a strong, reliable ally, other than Sawyer, had just monumentally blown up in her face.

"You're not going to interview Sawyer or Noah or take statements, are you?" she asked.

"I'll check into things and see if it needs to get that far."

If it needs to get that far. Piper wanted to scream. Instead, she politely rose from her wooden chair and even offered her hand.

"Nice to meet you, Sheriff Garcia."

She barely remembered saying it when she was back in her truck. Everything after *if it needs to get that far* was a blur. Trembling in fear and anger, she could not shake the unnerving feeling she was being watched. She jabbed her key into the ignition, took a deep breath, and pulled the hell out of the parking lot. It was only when she'd driven around the block and pulled the truck over that she hung her head in her hands and cried. Oblivious to who may see her. Did it really matter? The entire town disliked her and thought she was some sort of crazy, inept city slicker anyway.

Do you know how brave you are?... Are you going to give all this up?... Just because of a few setbacks...

When he first returned to the ranch, Sawyer's words echoed in her ears. Brave. Maybe, even though she wasn't so sure, she remained that way. Setbacks. She smiled through her tears before wiping them away. He sure had a penchant for understatement. Setbacks, my ass. She threw on her left turn signal and pulled back out into traffic, heading for the hospital to see how he'd fared. Maybe the doctor had stitched up his setbacks.

We're two underdog warriors, she thought, smiling more widely, despite her dire situation. Things really couldn't get much worse, could they?

Twenty-Two

SAWYER SAT BACK in his vinyl chair in the waiting room, getting as comfortable as he could, under the circumstances, trying his best to think of anything but the pain. His head throbbed much worse than the wound on his arm, despite the lidocaine injection they'd given him in the temple. He'd only needed six stitches there and, surprisingly, none in his arm. The doctor, a young resident who'd told him he was from Chicago, had looked at him skeptically when he explained the graze wound from the bullet.

"This sure looks like your friend was much closer to you than you say when he accidentally discharged his gun."

"Could be," Sawyer had shifted nervously, "like I said, I really wasn't looking at him while I replaced our targets."

The doctor had pretty much remained quiet after that as he disinfected and dressed the wound. Of course he's reluctant to believe me, Sawyer decided in the waiting room afterward. He's from Chicago, where the vast majority of people with gunshot wounds lie about where and how they got them. People aren't shot by accident in the big city during target practice. They're wounded or killed because of armed robberies and drug deals gone bad. And people in Cassidy Falls weren't shot at all.

His thoughts once again returned to Piper. He hadn't expected her to be gone this long. Although he hadn't said anything to discourage her, he was doubtful she'd get to see the Sheriff. Heck, he even doubted a deputy would take time out of his slow, uneventful day to take a report. Some things she has to find out for herself, he groaned. She wasn't the type of woman to be told the way things rolled by some man. Even her favorite ranch manager. He chuckled as he took out his phone.

I should text her, he thought before deciding against it. She'll get here when she gets here. The last thing he wanted to do was rush her and throw added tension and stress onto her plate. But isn't that what I've done, he thought reluctantly, by even coming back here? If not for my dogged insistence and intervention, she would have sold the ranch to Martinez by now. She'd be safe from Martinez's rage. And also free and clear of all the hard work and headaches that rebuilding and running the ranch entailed.

I'd be safe too, he acknowledged, still reeling as he wrapped his head around his own attempted murder. He'd come back to Cassidy Falls to straighten out his shattered and chaotic life. As much as he disliked considering it, and hated himself for even thinking it, he surmised it was probably best for all concerned that he leave.

After all, who could really blame him? He'd almost been killed. As he mournfully went over his departure plans, he couldn't shake the heart-wrenching vision of Piper's sad and defeated face. She'd been utterly devastated when she'd decided to sell before he returned, and she'd be crushed again when forced to sell after he deserted her again. Life was filled with complicated and difficult choices, and sometimes none were good.

"You trying to decide whether to go for the risky brain surgery or something?"

He jumped at Piper's voice. He'd been so deep in thought he hadn't noticed her walk up beside him.

"What do you mean?" he did his best to smile.

"The look on your face spells doom and gloom. Are you more injured than we first thought?"

"Nah," this time, his smile came easy. "Doctor's not even sure I have a concussion. But I'm going to have Tim and Will take turns waking me up every hour tonight just to play it safe. You get to see the Sheriff?" he asked quickly, grateful to steer the conversation away from himself.

"Sure did," she dragged out the words in a frustrated hiss. "Let's get out of here, and I'll tell you all about it."

Seated in her truck, he listened intently as she told him what had happened. He was annoyed but not completely surprised, except for the fact that she'd actually gotten to speak to Garcia. Now that had taken incredible perseverance and determination on her part. Feeling guilty all of a sudden for not telling her more about the Sheriff, he decided it was time to fill her in.

"Garcia and Martinez are good friends. I'm actually surprised the Sheriff was as polite to you as he was."

"Good friends?! You knew this and didn't tell me?" anger flushed her cheeks red.

"Sorry, ma'am, I reckon I should have. But you were so determined to see him and file a report that I figured you'd just be intimidated and more shaken than you already were."

His pitiful explanation didn't calm her. It fueled her rage instead. Why did men think it was all right to keep things from her in the heavens? To protect her perceived delicate emotions and fragile state of mind? Why on earth did they think that she was too irrational or too flighty to decide what to do? Or how to act after knowing all the facts?

"Firstly, Sawyer," she said through gritted teeth, "I would appreciate you not keeping anything from me in the future. A little more confidence in me would be nice." *He had called her brave when he first returned.* "Secondly," she continued, "we've almost just been killed together. I think that makes us close enough for you to drop the ma'am in favor of my first name."

He took a deep breath and sighed. Piper looked so pretty, so vibrant and determined, even in her anger. How could he even think of deserting her when she needed his help the most. If he up and left, he'd probably never see her again.

"Yes, ma'am...uh, Piper. It won't happen again. Full disclosure of everything from here on in, I promise."

"Speaking of that," she smirked as she started up the truck and slowly backed out of the parking spot, "did you tell the doctor the truth about what happened?"

"I said it was a target practice accident."

She groaned and glared at him.

"I figured I could always tell the truth later, depending on how your visit to the Sheriff's office went. Look," he leaned a little towards her, "no point making waves, causing problems, and starting rumors, if nothing's likely to be done anyway."

"And if the Sheriff does read over your medical report? How will that look?!" her voice raised.

"With all due respect, that isn't going to happen. You didn't grow up here, Piper. You'll learn soon enough, that's just not how things work around here."

She said nothing, putting on her blinker and carefully turning left onto Main Street, doing her best to ignore the chill up her spine.

Denton's Pharmacy was directly ahead of them, only a few blocks up on the right side. She suddenly realized that the doctor had probably given Sawyer a pain prescription. She asked him if they needed to stop.

"It's right here," he said, patting the right front pocket of his jeans. "But the last thing I need in my life are heavy-duty pain pills, so I'll be settling for some Tylenol when we get home."

"OK," she nodded understandingly.

No argument from her this time.

"But I am supposed to eat something right away," he remembered. "Doc told me I lost a bit too much blood. What do you say we stop at Bert & Barnie's Roadhouse? They got the best hot and spicy chicken wings this side of Dallas. My treat," he added with a smile.

"Sure," at just the mention of food Piper's stomach was rumbling.

She, too, needed a good meal and relaxation after the day they've had. She'd overheard the ranch hands talking about this roadhouse, and it honestly did seem like the best place at the moment to chill and calm her nerves.

Except it wasn't. She was wrong.

Twenty-Three

PIPER LOVED THE PLACE – its rustic exterior, engraved wooden sign, wagon wheel porch decorations – until they walked inside. Even before her eyes grew accustomed to the darkened interior, she was aware all eyes had instantly focused on them. And not in a good way. The place grew silent. Whispering started when the conversation resumed.

Her chest tightened and stomach was in knots. She was about to turn around when Sawyer gently placed his hand on her shoulder and encouraged her ahead.

"We don't seem too welcome here," she said quietly, but he just smirked.

"If you're gung-ho determined on staying here and making a life for yourself, you had better get used to being the odd one out for quite some time yet," he smiled, as he pulled out a chair for her and took a seat himself.

They'd chosen a quiet corner, fairly close to the bar and the kitchen, where a few empty tables surrounded them.

"What'll you guys have?"

At least the waitress was cheery. Sammy, as her name tag said, looked barely old enough to work in a bar. She either was inexplicably unaware of the rumors and animosity surrounding the newcomers, or she wanted a big fat tip enough to not care and play nice. It didn't matter which, Piper decided. Her stomach was still growling something awful, and whether other patrons liked it or not, she was damn well going to have a good meal, at least one very tall drink, and a good time.

"Get me a Blue Hawaiian, if your bartender knows how to make one, and also the Nachos with extra cheese, please."

Sawyer raised an eyebrow but said nothing other than placing his own order. He went for the extra hot and spicy chicken wings and whatever beer they had on tap.

"What?" she asked him, laughing when she couldn't get over the look on his face.

"I've seen you drink beer and wine and even whiskey. Somehow, you've never struck me as a Blue Hawaiian type of girl."

She furrowed her eyebrows, unsure of whether this was a compliment.

"Seems like you're not shying away from more attention," he leaned towards her, smiling. "I don't think anyone's ever ordered such a city slicker girlie drink in this bar before."

"Oh," she sighed with relief. "I figured they're already talking dirt about me and how I don't fit in here. I just thought I'd give them a little something more to talk about."

And talk they did. As obvious as their gossip was, it actually amused her. Maybe she was just giddy and defiant in the aftermath of near death. For whatever reason, Piper genuinely enjoyed being the center of attention, even if the attention wasn't in the least bit admiring or good. She enjoyed it, that is until the short-black-haired woman who'd insulted her at the auction walked in. She came to their table and insulted her again.

"Well, look who's here. Little miss sweet cheeks. Still haven't learned to leave ranching to the professionals? I would have thought you'd tucked your pretty little delicate tail between your legs and crawled back home to where you came from."

"How dare you!" Piper yelled.

She was on her third Blue Hawaiian, but in the mood that she was in, she would have responded the same way even before her first drink.

"I have no idea who you are or why you dislike me but listen here, you have no right to speak to me this way. You know nothing about me other than idiotic small-minded gossip and rumor, but that's fine. My life is certainly not your business anyway!"

"What I do know, sweet cheeks, is that your kind doesn't belong here. I do know that it's time for...."

"Enough!" Sawyer screamed and stood. "If you do not leave us alone this instant, I will personally escort you to another table, or straight the hell outside, whichever you prefer."

The bar went silent. For a frightening few seconds, Piper had the horrible feeling this little unpleasant exchange would escalate into a bar-wide brawl. But no one stood. No one spoke or even gestured. The black-haired woman turned on her heel and stomped her way over to the bar.

"Whiskey, straight up!" she yelled, and Piper noticed that the burly bartender already had it waiting.

"She must be a regular here," Piper said quietly, leaning towards Sawyer, who'd just sat back down.

"Looks like it. She does look familiar. I'm pretty darn sure she's the wife of Hernando Sanchez. He's one of Noah Martinez's good friends."

"Figures..." Piper scowled, then told Sawyer about her encounter with the woman at the auction.

"It was a setup," he shook his head. "To make you feel unwelcome and to convince you that cattle prices are out of your league. You don't have to spend that much money on each head when you first start off."

"Martinez will stop at nothing, but I guess we already know that after this afternoon," she frowned.

"Let's get out of here, Piper," he stood, walked up behind her, and pulled out her chair.

At least there's one man who's a gentleman towards me, Piper thought as they walked towards the lobby and the bar's outside doors. She was lost in thought about what just happened and still ranting about it to Sawyer when something on the wall in the lobby caught his eye. His photo. On a Wanted poster. He quickly ushered Piper through the doors before she had a chance to notice. The last thing she needed was yet another thing to worry about and more stress.

WANTED FOR TRESPASSING ON MARTINEZ RANCH.

Of course. Martinez needed a reason for shooting him. This scenario was the perfect coverup of wrongdoing, if anybody but Sheriff Garcia investigated it. The poster certainly wasn't there when they'd arrived at the bar. It must have been placed there quickly to see whenever they left. Everyone knows I've been in here, Sawyer pondered, so why not just come and arrest me on the spot? Then it hit him. What the poster is, is actually just a warning. Make problems for Martinez and wind up with your ass in jail.

"You've gone pretty quiet," Piper looked at him curiously, as they drove through town.

Quiet and shocked was actually more like it. The Wanted posters were everywhere: On telephone poles, store windows, and on the sides of post office letterboxes. He quickly turned to Piper and started chatting to keep her looking at him and occupied. He didn't feel any better once they'd driven out of town onto the first dirt road that led to her ranch. There were no posters to be seen, but his aversion to them was replaced by a threatening, ominous feeling.

This was only the beginning. Martinez wasn't done.

Twenty-Four

THE MENACING, depressing cloud of dread hung over Sawyer their entire way home. He did his best to cover up his uneasiness, but in the end, he realized he hadn't done a very good job.

"You're thinking Noah's going to come back and try to kill us, aren't you?" Piper asked him, as she pulled off the road to make her way up her long driveway.

He grimaced. In actuality, he really wasn't sure what to think. Noah was obviously past the point of thinking clearly in his frenzy to take over her ranch. He'd stop at nothing, but there was no way to predict his next move. All they could predict was that there *would* be a next move and things were likely to get much, much uglier from here on in.

"I think he's too smart to repeat his mistake. Not that he has any love for us and wouldn't jump for joy if we died, but in the end, I doubt it matters to him one way or the other. All he wants is your ranch, whether we're alive or dead."

"He did try to kill us, Sawyer!"

"Yes, but only in the spur of the moment, out of blind rage, when he realized you'd slipped out from under his influence and weren't going to sell. My guess is that he's going to come up with another plan," he said as they walked up the front porch steps. "I wouldn't worry about getting shot at or...."

He stopped mid-sentence and gasped, pulling her backward, so she was behind him. The front door was slightly ajar.

"What's..."

"Did you lock the door when we left?" his voice was tense.

"Of course, why?"

She pushed past him to see what he was looking at and let out a tiny, quiet shriek.

"Stay here," he urged. "There may be someone still inside."

"You're *not* going in there!" she whispered and grabbed his arm, attempting to guide him off the porch. "We're getting back in the truck, and I'm calling the police."

"That won't help, trust me," he said softly as he led her to the far side of the porch. "Duck around the other side of the house if you hear me confront somebody. Otherwise, just wait here till I come to get you."

He turned away quickly and slipped inside the door. And almost jumped out of his skin when he felt someone behind him. He spun to gaze into her fervent eyes.

"Not a chance. We're in this together. Let's look around."

Before he could stop her, she walked into the middle of the living room and yelled.

"If you're still in here, you better come out! We're armed!"

"Never, ever, and I mean this, Piper," he insisted a few minutes later once they'd determined the intruder had gone, "never pretend you have a weapon when you don't. It's a surefire way to get yourself killed."

"You're right," she sighed, "I'm sorry. I'm just so angry I can't think straight anymore."

He dropped the tea towels he'd been holding onto the table and rushed across the kitchen to her. His grip was gentle but firm on her wrists.

"Don't say that. You can't afford to become careless or lax. Not now, not when you've already come this far."

Her laugh was bitter and helpless. "Yeah, just look at everything I've accomplished. A burnt down barn, barely half-renovated house with not enough money to finish it, and now this super lovely décor."

She waved her arm around the kitchen and towards the living room. Her house had been totally trashed, and it would take them hours to clean things up. Of course, their first thought had been Noah, or one or more of his henchmen. But they had no proof and not even a clue as to what he'd been looking for. She had very few valuables except some jewelry from when she'd been with her husband, but these were worth peanuts compared to what Martinez could easily afford. He wasn't after riches. All he wanted was her ranch.

"We'll get this cleaned up and things figured out, don't you worry," Sawyer assured her. "Why don't you take another look around while I finish up in the kitchen and see if anything at all was stolen."

She huffed. "I've checked twice. They probably just didn't find whatever they were looking for."

"Then check a third time," Sawyer smirked. "Now that you've calmed down a little, you'll be able to think."

He was right. She wandered into the living room and began cramming bills and receipts, littering the floor back into her desk drawer. Shoving things aside to make room for them, she screamed. Her settlement papers! Why hadn't she noticed this before?! The details of John's financial settlement with her, his gift of the ranch, and the proof of its ownership being transferred to her. All of it was gone!

"Just calm down," Sawyer said gently as he handed her the cold glass of iced tea. He'd ushered her to the kitchen table so she could sit and collect herself. "All you have to do is get more copies of everything from your lawyer. It'll all be in your file."

She hung her head in her hands, elbows on the table, and cried.

"You don't understand. I barely had any money of my own when I was married. I didn't hire my own lawyer. I used John's because he said he'd take care of everything."

Not a smart move. He winced but kept his opinion quiet. He simply rubbed her shoulder comfortingly and told her to get her husband's lawyer to make copies then.

"Matthews is one of John's best friends. I have a very, very bad feeling, Sawyer, that he won't replace the paperwork. John was huffy about giving me the ranch and so much money, to begin with. Now that he's had more time to think...."

"Did you at least make copies of any of it yourself?" Sawyer asked.

"No," her face contorted. "I must be the most stupid woman alive! I shouldn't have trusted John to be fair and honest in the first place after he cheated on me!"

"You think John had your paperwork stolen, then?" he asked, gently taking her hands in his.

"I don't know what to think!"

Neither did he. With two dishonest people wishing she didn't have the ranch, with perhaps either of them capable of anything to take it away from her, their battle was all uphill. Still, as they sat and talked about it, they decided that Martinez was most likely behind the theft. Although not thrilled with having to provide her with a fair divorce settlement, her ex-husband hadn't made waves. Albeit grudgingly, he'd given in to her demands and, by all accounts, was thrilled to be free of her. The culprit behind the theft had to be her neighbor. If you were capable of murder, theft was a piece of cake.

"I've made mistakes, but none of this would have happened," she looked at him pointedly, "if you hadn't convinced me not to sell."

So they were back to that topic, I guess. She was frustrated, frightened, and depressed, so he forgave her anger. Merely nodding quietly as she ranted and raved. By the time they retired for the evening to try and get some restless sleep, they weren't even speaking. They communicated in quick, short comments when absolutely necessary as they finished cleaning the place up. Sawyer could hear her crying mournfully, sweeping the kitchen floor after Piper had gone upstairs to bed. He felt so guilty and helpless. He just had to think of something. He had to come up with a plan and a way to help.

Twenty-Five

WHEN HIS ALARM went off at 5:30 the next morning, Sawyer was already lying awake in bed. He'd spent most of the night tossing and turning, struggling to come up with a reliable and viable plan. Finally, as the night sky slowly faded into a dark shade of violet, he thought he had it all worked out. At least if everything went to plan. He'd tell Piper all about it over breakfast after they'd laid out the food for all the men. Although exhausted, he was actually full of energy when he leaped from his bed.

Despite their current obstacles and problems, he was determined to keep the ranch hands busy and forge ahead with construction, rebuilding the barn, and starting with repairing portions of the dilapidated pasture fence. Sitting at his small table in his bedroom, he wrote out the long list of supplies he'd pick up after breakfast. He hoped that his determination and positive attitude would rub off on Piper and that she'd be able to shake her depression and defeated attitude from the evening before.

His step was light and carefree as he strode into the kitchen about an hour later to begin preparing the food. Dejected that Piper wasn't downstairs to join him, he forced himself to think only positive thoughts. *Her mood will pick up as soon as I explain what I have* planned, he told himself over and over as he cracked egg after egg and poured the contents into multiple frying pans. The bacon was nearly ready, and all the toast and hash browns were done by the time the men began filing into the room.

"Smells fantastic, as always," Tim smiled as he pulled out a chair at the table. "How you feeling, buddy? Was there enough Tylenol in the world to get rid of your massive headache?" he laughed.

Jesus, Sawyer remembered! He'd meant to ask Tim and Will to wake him every hour, as per the doctor's instructions, to make sure he could wake and didn't have a concussion. No matter, really, he quickly concluded. He doubted he got anywhere near an hour's sleep in one stretch last night anyway. And luckily, he'd easily woken up multiple times.

"Yup, Tylenol worked great," he smirked. "So good; I wish I had stock in the company."

At this, all the men laughed, joking they would have soothed their pain with beer or whiskey instead. No one seemed to notice or care that Sawyer didn't take a seat at the table and eat with them. He'd put two plates aside, one for him, the other for Piper, so they could eat and talk as soon as she decided to come downstairs. Discouraging the men from clearing the table, he insisted they just get outside and to work instead. He'd given them a ton of tasks to keep them busy until he returned this afternoon with more supplies.

When Piper still hadn't come down for breakfast by the time he was placing the last washed dish in the rack, he began wondering whether he should go upstairs and gently tap on her bedroom door. For sure, she hadn't done anything truly crazy in her depression, but he hoped that she hadn't decided to get drunk. She'd need a clear head to listen to him and provide input concerning his plan.

Deciding against waking her – sure they were becoming closer friends, but she was still his boss – he made plans to run into town for supplies instead. Hopefully, she'd be awake by the time he returned. He was about to start his vehicle to pull out of the driveway when he decided to leave her a note. Tearing a sheet of clean-lined paper from his notepad, he scrawled some quick details. *Gone to town for supplies. Be back soon. Need to talk to you right away. I have a great plan!* Well, great if everything we need to accomplish it falls into place, he thought, as he placed the note conspicuously on the kitchen table. Please don't lose hope, Piper, he prayed as he left the room.

His trip to town was uneventful, despite his persistent, uneasy feeling that Sheriff Garcia or one of his deputies would jump out of the woodwork and slap cuffs on him. But no, just as he'd surmised the day before, the Wanted poster was merely a warning for him not to make waves about Martinez shooting at them. Adding to his relief about their predicament, he was overjoyed to see Piper sweeping the front porch as he pulled into their driveway. She must be feeling better. You don't sweep your home if you've given up on it. He jumped from his truck to go talk to her, even before he took the supplies he'd purchased to the men.

"You get my note?" he asked cheerfully.

"Yes," her expression was barely lukewarm.

"Just let me take this stuff to the guys, and then we'll have a late breakfast, and I'll fill you in on everything. I saved two plates for us."

He stood staring at her until she acknowledged what he had just said. No smile. Just a nod, but at least she didn't run off back upstairs to wallow in self-pity in her room.

"It will work, trust me. Martinez is greedy. He'll take the bait."

Sawyer told her a few minutes later as they sat across from each other at the kitchen table, their reheated breakfasts steaming in front of them.

She'd made a fresh pot of coffee before he'd gotten back to the house. That was a good sign, she planned on sitting and talking for a while.

"Yes, he's greedy, but he's not stupid. Why would he believe for even a second that I've miraculously changed my mind and want to sell? Especially, of all people, to him!"

"Because," Sawyer smiled, taking a big bite of his toast, "he'll *want* to believe you because he wants this ranch so much."

"But still," she sighed, "we're assuming he'll come back here to visit. That's a huge assumption. I'd sure never set foot on this property again if I were him."

"Because if you were him, you'd think like a rational human being, not motivated by self-interest and greed."

She took a long, delicious sip of her coffee. Sawyer had a point. The only hope she had of holding on to her ranch long-term, and avoid conflicts and additional expenses due to vandalism, was to outwit Noah at his own game. If only she had more practice at being devious and dishonest! Until her separation from her husband, she didn't recall any serious situation where she'd actually stood up for herself before. Maybe with Sawyer's help and support, she thought as she smiled at him, she could actually pull this off.

He didn't say anything about how much her smile buoyed him and warmed his heart. It had tortured him seeing her so defeated and distraught. Especially because she'd blamed him, whether that was totally fair or not. The important thing was that her situation wasn't so hopeless and desperate anymore. They had a plan. A real, honest to goodness, workable plan. All they had to count on was Noah's insatiable greed. And that, at least, was a certainty.

Twenty-Six

A FULL TWO weeks had gone by, and they neither heard nor saw any sign of Noah. Sawyer began to think he'd been wrong. Not about the fact that Noah was greedy. That would never change. But wrong about the fact that he would actually show up again at the ranch. Maybe he figures we've all armed ourselves and are just itching for a reason to retaliate. Whatever the case, he decided they couldn't wait forever. There was no telling what he would do with Piper's stolen papers and no way to predict what despicable, evil acts he had up his sleeve. No, he and Piper had to be proactive. Thwart Noah's actions and, instead, make him play their game. He brought it up to Piper when she came out to the barn with fresh, homemade lemonade.

Pulling her aside so the men couldn't hear, he explained what he had in mind.

"This afternoon?!" Piper stared at him like a deer in headlights. "Maybe we should wait a bit longer before we do anything."

"No," Sawyer shook his head. "We don't want to give him any more time to do whatever damage he plans to with your paperwork."

Huffing, Piper agreed.

"Look," he said, "I know you're nervous. But trust me, you'll easily be able to pull this off. Think of it as tricking a very hungry pig that's rooting for food. It has a one-track mind, just like Martinez. Getting it to do what you want is easy when you dangle that pail of feed in front of its face."

"My ranch is the feed," Piper smirked.

"Exactly. Hurry up and get ready. I'll get washed up, and we'll head into town."

Bert & Barnie's Roadhouse was as busy as ever when they arrived. Ignoring the curious glances their way, Piper and Sawyer chose a table for two, smack in the middle of the room this time. They wanted everyone to overhear their private conversation. Sawyer forced himself to contain his burgeoning smile, looking around as inconspicuously as he could as he pulled the chair out for Piper. Besides the bartender on duty, he noted at least three of Noah's friends and associates. He supposed it wasn't sheer luck. After all, Noah was well-liked and respected and had ties of some sort with just about everybody in this town.

"What'll you have?" a different waitress than before had strolled to their table.

"I'm in the mood for a double patty burger with lots of bacon and cheese today," he smiled. "Fries on the side and whatever beer you have on tap will do just fine."

She scrawled his order on her notepad without even looking at it. She had her eyes trained on Piper instead.

"Same for me, but oh, maybe just a single patty burger, thanks."

She nodded curtly and spun to walk away.

"We're certainly not the most popular people in town, are we?" Piper smirked as she leaned across the table, closer to him.

"That's what I'm counting on," he laughed. Then speaking quietly, he said, "They're all so anxious to gather dirt and talk crap about us, they'll strain to hear our every word. Let's just chat about the weather or something for a few minutes before we get down to business."

She nodded and immediately began complaining about how hot it was outside.

After a few quick exchanges on the topic, she finally said as loud as she could, "I honestly don't know how you can stand to work outside in this heat all day."

"Just used to it, I guess. I grew up on a ranch. I'm really going to miss working for you, ma'am, once you sell your ranch."

He saw four or five heads turn towards them, and that was only what he could see out of the corner of his eyes.

"I'm sorry. I'm really going to miss Baker Ranch myself, but honestly, I don't see what else I can do. I'm out of money. Like you said earlier, it would take a miracle for me to hold it together here long enough to build up any substantial income from cattle. Dammit, and now with Noah's offer off the table, I've also lost my chance at a really lucrative sale. Thank God I have some other offers. Something is better than nothing," she did her best to look forlorn.

By the time they left the roadhouse about forty minutes later, they had noticed that many of the other patrons had spent an unusual amount of time on their phones. Bingo, Sawyer smiled. At least one, if not many of them, had already been yapping their heads off to Martinez.

Now it was just a waiting game.

Twenty-Seven

BRIGHT AND EARLY THE next morning, they realized they hadn't had long to wait. The men had just finished breakfast and gone outside. Piper and Sawyer were stacking the washed dishes in the rack when they heard a vehicle coming up her drive. After rushing to peek out her front window, Sawyer returned with a triumphant smile.

"It's him. Don't worry, you've got this!" he added when she flinched. "Think of him as an easily manipulated, hungry pig," he laughed as he ducked out the back door.

Clinging to that vision actually did calm her nerves, as she made her way to the front door. He was already knocking when she got there, and she made sure to plaster the congenial look on her face as she opened the door.

"Noah!" she managed to feign surprise quite well.

"Hello little miss...uh, Ms. Baker," he quickly corrected himself.

It wouldn't do for him to be so condescendingly friendly after what he had said and done. In silent amusement, she watched him struggle to adjust the expression on his face. Voila! From patronizing and chauvinistic to repentant and apologetic in a mere second or two.

"Please, would you be so kind as to allow me in?"

She hesitated just long enough to make him worry, then stepped back as she swung the door open wider.

"I can't even imagine what brings you here after our little *incident*. But far be it from me to be the one to continue our disagreement. Coffee?" she turned her head to ask as he followed her quietly into the kitchen.

"Yes, please. I would appreciate one so early in the morning," he smiled.

"So, what brings you here this early?" she asked innocently, as she pulled two mugs from her cupboard.

"An apology."

She turned to stare at him. Stammering for a moment, he continued. He clearly wasn't used to apologizing to anyone for anything.

"I deeply regret my harsh words and actions. I'm afraid my emotions got the better of me. With my wife gone, you see, my life has been in turmoil. I had hoped to expand my ranch by purchasing yours, to throw myself deeper into my work. Bury my sorrows, so to speak."

"I see."

"I would like to think we can still remain friends," his smile looked almost genuine. "Being neighbors, after all, I will help you out any way I can."

I just bet, she thought, but kept her expression neutral. It was time to dangle the bait and reel him in.

"That's very kind of you, Noah, but unfortunately, it's a little too late for that. I mean, as far as helping me to rebuild this ranch and remain here. I'm so miserable," she said as she placed their coffee on the table and took her seat. "Despite what's happened, I do have to admit that you were right and that your advice was accurate. I'm simply in over my head and have decided to sell. I've been looking over some offers...."

"Offers?" he squirmed in his chair.

Yes, offers, she wanted to scream. As if he didn't know. That's why he was here. The town gossips had already filled him in.

"Yes, I have a few and will be making my decision by tomorrow evening. It's really best that I leave here and get a fresh start somewhere else."

"Your employees are still working on the barn," he said a little suspiciously. "I'm a bit confused...."

She had to think quickly. She and Sawyer hadn't thought of this!

"Well, yes," she sighed after a moment, "each of the offers expressly states their purchase is conditional upon my rebuilding the barn."

"I can do better than that!" his face gleamed. "My original offer stands as it was, except, of course, if you receive something higher. Then I will top it. But I am willing to take Baker Ranch off your hands as is."

"My goodness!"

"Yes, and I sorely hope it helps me make amends for my ill-mannered actions of late."

How kind of you, she thought sarcastically, seething, but smiled.

"Thank you, Noah. You are very generous. I would be happy to sell Baker Ranch to you."

His benevolent expression melted into something more animated. He wasn't very good at hiding his surprise. He was the very last person, he thought, that she would ever sell to. It's a good thing for financial problems and desperation, he mused, struggling to smother his smile.

"I will get the newly-dated offer to you as soon as possible," he stood and held his arm towards her to shake her hand.

"Marvelous," she shook his hand firmly and chatted with him pleasantly as she walked him to the door. "Thank goodness," she added as an afterthought, once he'd walked out the threshold, "that I still have all of my documents pertaining to this property. I've had some of the worst luck. There was a robbery while I was away the other day, but the documents they stole relating to my property were fakes."

Noah's eyes widened. He said nothing for a moment, then gathered his composure and shook his head.

"How prudent of you to have fakes created. Was there a specific reason, may I ask?"

"Well," she sighed, "only that my divorce and settlement were a bit contentious. I thought it best to keep all of the original, real paperwork in a safe place."

"Ah, yes of course," this time, his complimentary smile was far from near genuine.

But Piper pretended she thought it was. Waving to him cheerfully as he turned his truck around to head out of her driveway, she made sure not to look too conspicuously at the cargo bed. It held a huge toolbox, a few hay bales, and some larger, tarped objects over to the side. That, she thought, is particularly handy.

She thought of Sawyer and said a little prayer.

Twenty-Eight

SO MUCH FOR A SMOOTH RIDE, Sawyer groaned as Noah raced over another bump. His truck was worth at least seventy-five thousand dollars, but you sure wouldn't know it if you were riding outside in the cargo bed breathing in dust and gravel, struggling to breathe under the filthy tarp. Judging by the way he was driving – angry and upset – he was heading straight home to pull Piper's documents out from wherever he had them safely hidden. There was no way he could resist having a closer look at them. And all I have to do, Sawyer mused, is make sure I somehow find a way to watch him, so I know exactly where to steal them back from.

After they'd been on the road for at least ten minutes, he realized that in all likelihood, Noah was not heading straight home. Although their ranches were large, they were still side by side, and they'd been driving awhile. From the motion and feel of the ride, he could tell that Noah was still speeding on the gravel road. He grimaced and hoped they weren't heading into town. He was tarped, but still, someone could spot him, maybe even Noah himself. If he decided to get something out of the back and move the tarp...

He forced himself to stay as calm as he could. If he was caught, he was caught. There was nothing he could do about it now. Despite his resolve to remain clear-headed and rational, he was actually wrestling with two very unsavory visions by the time Noah skidded his truck to a stop. Vision One: Staring down the barrel, yet again, of Noah's gun. Two: Being dragged, cuffed and uncooperative, by Sheriff Garcia and unceremoniously tossed into jail. Neither suited his fancy, but he decided a cell was definitely preferable to a grave. They were in town, he could tell by the noise of the traffic and voices of people as they chatted nearby.

"Noah! I wasn't expecting you. What's up?" he'd caught his attorney in the parking lot heading out for some meeting or maybe an early lunch.

"Let's go into your office, Jeb. I need a purchase offer for Baker Ranch typed up right away so I can sign and deliver it."

Jeb Lawson sighed. Any client other than Noah Martinez, he could put off for a few hours, at least until he'd had his lunch.

"OK, but you do know that you're interfering with my grumbling stomach and my exceptionally serious need this afternoon for a very stiff drink. Just got off the phone, conference call from hell."

"I don't have food but a good drink I can sure supply you with. I just bought a case of whiskey, Johnnie Walker, yesterday. Let me grab a bottle. The case is still in the back of my truck."

Sawyer cringed. Suddenly, he was aware of how loud his breathing sounded and how much his chest moved with each breath. Still and silent, he willed. With any luck at all, Martinez would not lift the tarp. Too afraid to so much as turn his head to look around himself, he had no idea whether the case of whiskey was tarped along with him or somewhere else in the bed of the truck. His breath hitched as the tarp moved close to his left foot. He caught a glimpse of Noah's hand just as his lawyer spoke.

"Never mind, Noah. I've already got an open bottle of Johnnie Walker in my desk's bottom drawer."

Sawyer hadn't even realized he'd been shakily holding his breath until he let it out as quietly as possible when the tarp settled back into place. He had no idea how long he laid there, curled uncomfortably under the tarp in the blazing heat. More than once, he'd thought of simply crawling out stealthily from underneath it and leaving, but where would that leave Piper? They'd lose the chance to locate her documents and steal them back. After one of the longest hours of his life, he finally recognized Martinez's heavy footsteps and heard him grunt as he settled in behind the wheel. Let's just hope there are no more pit stops. Sawyer sneered and tried to get a little more comfortable to handle the bumps in the road.

By the time Noah finally slowed down and pulled off the gravel, Sawyer was wondering whether they were going straight back to Piper's place. After all, Noah was in a big hurry to drop off his purchase offer so Piper could sign. If that's the case, he moaned. I've got a much longer wait under this tarp before Noah heads home. Piper would have to come up with valid, believable excuses as to why she wasn't signing back the offer right away. He had confidence in her, she could do it, but he wasn't looking forward to the additional delay.

After a couple of minutes, Sawyer decided that, surprisingly, Martinez had actually returned to his ranch. He could tell by the twists and turns he took as he drove up the driveway. Piper's driveway was more or less straight. The truck skidded to a stop, and he heard Noah jump out. His footsteps were heavy, angry as he walked away briskly from the front of his truck. Now or never, Sawyer groaned as he quickly crawled out from under the tarp and peaked his head over the side of the cargo bed.

Martinez was heading to a small cottage close to his house. As soon as he burst through the door, Sawyer rushed quietly up the path and dropped to his knees in front of the cottage's closest open window. Raised voices resonated from inside as he watched three men arguing with such intensity he thought they'd resort to fists.

"Job, is this why I pay you so much damn money?!" Noah screamed. "Can't you do anything right?"

"Noah, what are you talking about?" asked the tall man in the suit, the one Sawyer didn't recognize.

"Seems my not-so-competent ranch hand has stolen fake documents from that bitch. She has the real copies safely stowed away somewhere."

Job's expression crumbled, and he stammered to speak until his cheeks were almost as red as Martinez's entire face. He snatched a thick, manila envelope off the corner of the desk.

"That's impossible, Noah. I looked at these papers before I took them. Everything you said you wanted. All the details are here."

"Of course, they are, you idiot! Fake details. What would be the point of creating fakes if they didn't look like the real thing?!"

Job's fingers shook as he struggled to open the envelope before the man in the suit snatched it from his grasp.

"So much for you keeping up your end of the bargain, Noah!" the suited man screamed.

"Don't blame me. Blame my imbecile of an employee here!"

Noah grabbed the envelope from the man and slammed it back down on the desk.

"Garbage! Nothing but useless trash to fuel my fireplace tonight!"

Sawyer gasped. Not particularly loudly, but loud enough to alert the men he was there. They turned their heads.

Twenty-Nine

SAWYER STUMBLED backward and took off running. How could I be this stupid, he thought, to make noise at the worst possible time?! He was running blindly, and he knew it. Still, it was preferable to slowing down, giving up, and getting caught. How clearly did they see me, he wondered, as he glanced around for the best place to hide. Noah's old hay barn was up past the cottage, about six hundred yards or so, and he headed there. By the looks of it, Noah had stopped using it, preferring to store his hay and straw in the much larger, more modern barns he'd had built.

He raced through the partially opened sliding door and skidded to a stop when he got inside. Just great, he grimaced. This section of the barn was a large, airy, wide-open room. Discarded bales of old hay scattered on the main floor, and equally ancient straw bales littered the upstairs semi-open loft. First place they'll look for me, he cringed as he scrambled up the old wooden ladder, but he really didn't have much choice. Expecting to hear running footsteps and raised voices any second, he leaped and crawled over bales to get to the farthest corner. Struggling to catch his breath by then, Sawyer tossed a few bales aside to make room, then pulled them back on top of himself.

They were heavy and awkward, and his chest and arms and legs ached from their weight. He struggled to calm and slow his breathing, afraid the men would hear him if they came inside and got too close. To his amazement, the world around him had grown silent. Thank God for head starts. In the few moments it took Noah and his buddies to race out the door and around the corner of the cottage to where he'd been at the window, they'd obviously lost sight of him. They'd taken off running, at first, in the wrong direction. Never thinking of splitting up. Never considering their intruder would race further onto the property rather than attempt to run off of it.

Sawyer stiffened when within a few minutes, he heard raised voices, muffled by the men's running footsteps. They stopped just outside the barn.

"Damn it, Job! Where in the hell did that asshole go?"

It was Noah, and he was much angrier than he'd been during the men's argument.

"You see who it was?"

That voice, Sawyer recognized as the mystery man in the cottage. He smirked. He's not going to be thrilled to get dust and dirt on that very expensive suit.

"No," Job sneered. "He was just a blur as he moved away."

"Doesn't matter," Noah huffed. "I have a really good idea who it was anyway. Must be the idiot that bitch has working for her. That handyman turned ranch manager. This is connected to Piper, I'm sure. Who else would she get to spy on us? She doesn't have a friend or ally in this town."

"Never mind guessing, let's just find the prick!" the suited man yelled.

Breathing a sigh of relief as their footsteps headed away from the barn, Sawyer flinched as the men stopped moving once again.

"He couldn't have gotten far, or we'd have seen him running," Noah concluded. "We better search this barn before we look anywhere else."

Lying as quiet and still as humanly possible, Sawyer listened as the men ambled inside. Have I left signs of my entry, he agonized? My footsteps on the dirt floor? Did I move anything?

"Check that part of the building, Job," Noah ordered, "and we'll take the rest of the main floor first."

Just great, Sawyer sighed. It sounded like Noah had plans to search not just the bottom floor but the entire barn. After a few minutes of listening to the men grumbling and complaining as they moved things around, Sawyer smirked as he heard the suited man whine.

"It's God damn dark in here, Noah. Can't you turn on some lights?"

"Don't use this building anymore," Noah snapped. "Had the power disconnected a long time ago. Just pull up your big boy pants there, bud, and use the flashlight on your cell phone if you're scared of the dark."

"Very funny. I just don't feel like tripping on something and breaking my neck."

"Or dirtying up your suit," Noah muttered once Sawyer heard his companion's footsteps walk away.

Their frustrated searching and quibbling would have actually been funny if the situation wasn't so grim. And I don't always have the best luck in the world, Sawyer pondered as he listened. What are the odds I'll be so lucky that Noah sends the inept Mr. I Don't Want To Dirty Up My Suit upstairs to the loft to look for me? It seemed like they were examining every inch of the barn. What felt like an hour, but was actually only about twenty minutes, finally concluded their main floor search when Job returned.

"All clear, Noah. You guys find any signs of him here?"

"Nope. But we're not done looking. Get upstairs and check the loft."

With each creak of every rung on the ladder, Sawyer held his breath as he heard Job climb up. Is he smart enough to think of not just shining his flashlight on the bales but moving them around as well? We're sure going to find out, Sawyer braced himself. At first, Job was hunting around in the loft's far corner, and yup, by the sounds of it, he'd really thought of moving the bales. But is he moving them to access all the areas or to see if I'm hiding underneath? It didn't much matter, he quickly concluded. Either way, if he moves the bales I've got piled on top of me, I'm screwed.

"How's it going up there?" Noah's gruff voice was tense and irritated.

"Well, how d'ya think?" Job snipped back. "If you want me to take a good look up here, it's going to take some time. You two are welcome to come up and help me."

"Insolent bastard," Noah muttered. "Must be paying him too much. He suddenly seems to think he has a right to talk back to me and voice an opinion too!"

By the time Job neared the area of the loft where he lay hidden, Sawyer's legs and chest were literally numb from the weight on top of him. As he listened to Job's slow and determined footsteps, he held his breath as he heard him slide and toss some bales. Just shine your stupid flashlight in my corner and conclude I'm not here, he willed. Silence that lasted an eternity. Then finally, more footsteps, walking away.

"Nothing!" he heard Job exclaim. The ladder creaked under his weight as he descended.

"Well, he's got to be here someplace," Noah sneered. "Let's get out of here and keep looking. He must have run into one of the other buildings."

Sawyer lay quietly for another few minutes, even after he heard them bickering as they went out the door. It would be just his luck if they decided to return. Eventually, he slowly moved the closest bale off of him. Then, when nothing happened, the next one, and the next. When, finally, he crawled out from underneath the last few bales covering his legs, he limped to the nearest loft window and peered outside. The men were just entering one of the equipment buildings. *It was important to note* that none of them carried the envelope with Piper's documents, he thought with a smile. In their rush to catch him, they'd left it behind.

Thirty

MOVING AS QUICKLY as his aching legs would allow, Sawyer rushed to the ladder and descended from the loft. Running across the barn's floor level to the still-open sliding door, he grunted from the sharp pains stabbing at his right leg. The bales had been heavy, and he'd been lying so awkwardly that he guessed he'd pulled a muscle somehow. The last thing he needed, but there was no time to worry about injury or pain.

Stepping out into the bright sunlight, he hesitated only a second before inching against the side of the building to its corner so he could peek around. He saw nothing but cattle grazing peacefully in the distance, fat, and content in their fields. No sign of Noah or his cohorts. Take your time in the equipment buildings, he thought, as he took off running back towards the cottage and Piper's paperwork.

The men had left instantly when they'd noticed him, so it was almost certain they'd simply left her documents discarded on the desk. Especially since they believed them to be useless fakes. Grab them and go. His mind was racing. It'll just take me a second, and it'll be smooth sailing from here. He believed it right up until the time he skidded to a stop at the cottage's front door. He grasped the doorknob to turn it, but it didn't budge. The door was locked.

Damn it! He couldn't believe his sorry luck. Even in their frenzy to catch him, one of the men had thought to quickly lock the door. Glancing around to make sure the men still weren't anywhere in sight, he rushed to the open window he'd been peering in. Entry was entry, no matter which way it was accomplished. Luckily, he'd removed and reinstalled many a window screen, so he was remarkably quick at taking this one-off. He crawled inside.

He'd never been so happy to see a manilla envelope in his life. Snatching it up and turning to rush out the door, he realized he'd better take a few moments to make sure he had everything that Piper needed back. He shook the envelope, partially sliding out the papers so he could leaf through them. She hadn't told him specifics about what was stolen and the exact number of documents. Still, by the looks of it, everything necessary was there. He'd just fumbled the papers back into the envelope when he was startled by a loud knock at the door.

"Job, you there?" the man sounded angry.

He knocked again.

"Stupid idiot," the man sneered. "Never around when there's backbreaking work to be done and when we could use his help."

Sawyer exhaled loudly and the voice trailed away as the man shuffled off. Maybe it was a good thing after all that the door was locked. He'd have been caught red-handed inside Job's cottage with no rational excuse or reason to be in there. He could have lied or simply been pushed by the man and left, but he didn't need the added drama. All he wanted was to get home safely in one piece. Which brought him to his next dilemma. How was he going to get there fast?

Noah's property, like Piper's, was huge. Aside from his house and clusters of barns and outbuildings near it, his ranch consisted of flat, open fields. That meant no cover. And that meant being seen and possibly shot at again. He had no idea whether Noah or the other men carried a weapon. Would they have had time to grab their guns? Knowing Noah, he huffed. *He probably walked around already armed. I don't have much choice,* he quickly concluded. *It's either run through the farm fields and pastures or up the gravel road.*

Rushing out the door, he leaned towards the idea of taking the gravel road. At least it was public, and if cars were driving by, it lessened the chances of Noah taking aim. But that was still the long way home, and, he sighed, the road was pretty dead. Through the fields, it had to be. He was running around the side of the cottage when he heard voices again. The men returned, and he had nowhere to dart and take cover. Except for the way he got here, in the back of Noah's truck.

He rushed up the path to get to it and nearly stumbled and fell from the pain. The more he ran or even moved, the more his pulled muscle ached. Grimacing as he crawled into the back of Noah's truck, he scowled at the sight of the filthy tarp. He'd thought he was done with it, but that's not how his luck went. How long would he possibly have to hide there? As it turned out, much, much longer than he thought.

It was getting close to dinner time, and the ranch came to life with workers on their breaks. He'd been wondering where Noah and the men had disappeared to when he heard Noah's grating voice close by.

"Don't worry. We'll get to the bottom of this soon enough and get it all fixed up."

"I'm getting sick and tired of your promises and excuses, Noah," it was the suited man.

"I assure you, we'll be right back on track sooner than you think."

Sawyer missed the rest of their conversation when it was drowned out by laughing and talking ranch hands on their way to grab something to eat. A few minutes later, his heart skipped a beat when he heard Noah jump into the driver's seat and start the truck. If he's going to see Piper, Sawyer gritted his teeth...but calmed down when he realized the drive was short and sweet. He'd probably just moved his vehicle up into his own driveway. Now all he had to do was wait until it was safe to crawl out from under the tarp and make a run for it.

It took a while for things to grow quiet. He listened to a multitude of visitors going up to Noah's door, with many being let inside to chat. They were all employees needing further instructions on tasks and more details about Noah's numerous projects by the sounds of it. Seems he was even a much busier and more ambitious man than either he or Piper first thought. By the time Sawyer's surroundings grew quiet, and he was able to crawl out quietly from under the tarp, the sun had almost disappeared from the horizon to be replaced by the nearly full moon.

Piper will be so worried, Sawyer agonized, picturing her nervously pacing in her kitchen and around her living room. And he knew exactly what she must be thinking. That Noah had somehow caught him and shot him once again. Maybe fatally this time. Doing his best to calm himself by envisioning Piper's happy expression when he got home – with her stolen documents to boot – Sawyer cautiously leaped from the back of the truck and headed back towards the old hay barn. By his estimates, the fields directly behind it were the quickest way to reach the fence line and get onto Piper's property. At least now he had the fast-arriving darkness to shield his presence and help him hide.

The quiet mooing of the cattle startled him more than once. He knew they were there in the fields, of course, but he'd been so intent on rushing home that he kept forgetting to stay clear of them, or at least as far away as he could. Cows with calves at their side could be downright dangerous, especially to strangers creeping around them in the dark. Sawyer glanced quickly to his left and right as he made his way through the relatively high grasses, hoping that nothing worse would come out of the shadows. Like a bull with his herd to protect.

Finally, he came upon the fencing separating Noah's property from Piper's. It was now so dark out he had to remove his cell from his pocket to shine its flashlight to see. He'd had enough problems and injuries today. The last thing he needed was to get snagged as he climbed over. But that wasn't likely, he realized, gasping. The portion of fencing directly in front of him had been cut. A small section was curling on itself, leaving a clean and neat pathway between both farms. *Son of a...* He very clearly remembered repairing this section of sagging fence with his helpers not that long ago. The breach in the fence was new and deliberate. Why was he not surprised?

Thirty-One

"SAWYER!" Piper's face lit up as soon as she saw him. She leaped from her seat at the kitchen table, nearly spilling her mug of hot chocolate as she stood. "My goodness, I was going insane already, wondering where you were. I had this horrible feeling that...that..." she stammered as her expression darkened.

She couldn't finish, but it didn't matter. Sawyer knew what she was going to say.

"I'm fine, Piper. I was just held up a few times, is all."

He did his best to appear light-hearted and relaxed, even though he was anything but. To quickly lift her spirits, he waved the manilla envelope in the air as he crossed the room.

"Oh my God, you got them! You really, truly got them back!" her smile lit the room.

"Yes, ma'am, I surely did," he grinned, extending his arm to give the envelope to her, but she didn't take it.

Instead, she flew forward and pulled him in for an enthusiastic hug. Feeling awkward for a second, he didn't know whether to embrace her back. Focused on how wonderful it was to have her in his arms, he finally relented and pulled her even closer, wrapping his arms protectively around her shoulders as she sighed.

"Thank you so very much!" she gushed as she finally released him, stepping back.

"No problem at all," he smiled, thinking all the while what a huge, dangerous problem it had been.

But, as they sat down together at the kitchen table, he also realized he didn't mind. At least not entirely. While he didn't crave danger or have a death wish of any sort, he did want to make Piper happy, to ensure she had everything she needed and that she was safe.

"What took you so long? I was actually at the point of trying to decide who to call."

"Call?" Sawyer raised an eyebrow. "I hate to remind you, but Sheriff Garcia should be at the bottom of your list. And there really is no one else."

"I know," her face clouded as she looked down. "That's what frightened me the most."

Deciding to change the topic for a little while, to give her a chance to completely calm down and realize they were both safe and back on track at the moment, he looked around the room as he decided what to talk about.

"Hot chocolate," he said, eyeing her mug.

"What? Oh, yes. Do you want one? It'll just take me a minute...."

"It's a mighty warm night for you to be enjoying such a hot drink."

"Oh," she chuckled. "I love it on really cold nights, but also, ever since I was a little girl, I drink it when I'm upset or scared. For some reason, I find it comforting, and it helps me to relax."

By the tense expression she had on her face when he walked in, her hot chocolate hadn't done the trick. But he didn't want to focus on that. Instead, he asked her to check over the envelope's contents to make sure that all her missing paperwork was there. Watching her as she sorted and leafed through it, he was struck by just how defenseless and vulnerable she was. She was a bright light in a dark world. She was much too innocent and trusting. He'd have to encourage her to get her own lawyer and certified copies of the documents and to keep everything in a safe place this time.

"All here," she said, elated. "Oh, Sawyer, I really don't know how to tell you how grateful I am. I can never, ever thank you enough."

Even as she said it, she cringed at the painful memory of how she'd treated him after the robbery. Blaming him for it. Telling him it never would have happened if he hadn't talked her out of selling her ranch to Martinez. She wanted so much to apologize, but in her distress, she just couldn't find the right words. He found them for her, in his own way.

"Like I said, no problem at all. Piper, I know you're grateful and also that you've been under a tremendous amount of stress. Please don't feel the need to thank me. Don't worry about any uncomfortable disagreements we've had."

She let out a deep breath. He'd done it again. Made everything seem so simple, so neatly taken care of, perfectly packaged while calmly and chivalrously pushing aside any and all mistakes and bad behavior on her part. As she sat, secretly thinking about how long he would continue to come to her rescue, he reassuringly sat across from her, wondering the same thing.

I've risked my life twice now for Piper, he considered. First, when Noah shot at us, and today, I retrieved her paperwork. But for some reason, he couldn't imagine doing anything else. Suddenly feeling incredibly guilty for running out on her shortly after she'd hired him, he resolved that he'd never desert her again. At least, as long as she truly and honestly wanted him around.

She stood to take her now-empty mug to the sink. Still deep in thought about his emotions as he watched her walk across the room, Sawyer realized his feelings for her were fast becoming more than friendship. Almost as if seeing her for the first time, he realized how enchanting and beautiful she was. He quickly reminded himself that her feelings for him were likely just platonic. She was still recovering from a nasty divorce; a new relationship was probably the furthest thing from her mind.

"Can I make you something to eat?" She turned around and was leaning against the sink. "You must be starving by now. Besides, I want you to fill me in about what took you so long to get back here today."

Not wanting to be a burden, Sawyer offered to make them both a quick bite when she admitted she hadn't eaten anything yet either. He detailed his not-so-thrilling adventures as he threw their bread in the toaster and flipped their ham and cheese omelet.

"My God, Sawyer! Do you think they had guns?"

He shook his head glumly.

"I really don't know, and I wasn't about to stick around or get caught to find out."

"So, they believed the documents they stole from me were fakes?"

"Yup. You should have heard Noah screaming at Job about it. But," his face grew serious, "I sincerely doubt they believe that anymore. Why would someone steal *fake* paperwork back?"

"Right," she looked sullen and distraught again. "And you have no idea who the other guy is? The one in the suit?"

"Nope. I've never seen him before, and he certainly isn't from around these parts. That much was obvious."

Eating their dinner a few minutes later, Sawyer gently introduced the idea of her getting her own lawyer, certified copies of the documents, and keeping them in a safe place. To his surprise, she was very receptive and eager to get it done. I suppose this horrible experience has taught her a lesson, he mused, to be much more careful about what she does and whom she trusts. He just hoped that she would retain her sweet love of life, her brave and adventurous nature, and her captivating inborn spunk.

Thirty-Two

THE NEXT DAY, Piper was up earlier than usual, even before Sawyer. When he arrived in the kitchen to begin making breakfast for the men, she was already there, humming to herself cheerfully and flipping over the eggs in frying pans.

"Well, looks like you've been awake even before the roosters could crow," he smiled at her, pleasantly surprised.

"We don't have any roosters," she laughed.

"Not yet, but we will soon enough," he smirked as he grabbed bread from the fridge and began putting slices in the toasters.

He guessed her good mood and bountiful energy resulted from getting her documents back. That was only part of it, as it turned out. His advice last night had had a significant effect on her outlook on life.

"I've already googled local divorce attorneys," she said, "and left a voicemail to make an appointment with one that seems like he'd be a good fit. I'll have him arrange certified copies of the documents, and, for now, he'll keep what I already have in a safe place. I'm heading into town today to run errands anyway, so I hope he squeezes me in."

"I hope he does too," Sawyer smiled. "I have to run to town myself for supplies, so there's no sense in us going separately. We can go together and maybe grab a quick bite at Bert & Barnie's Roadhouse if there's time."

"I'd love that."

They'd just finished breakfast with the men and begun the dishes when Piper's cell phone rang. It was the attorney's secretary, and Piper ran into the living room to grab some paper and a pen. She returned to the kitchen, beaming.

"I have to be at James Garrett's office in an hour."

"Perfect. You go get ready. I'll just finish the dishes and get changed."

Although they took Piper's truck because it was bigger, Sawyer drove. The plan was to drop her off at the lawyer's, grab as many supplies as he could before she called, then pick her up and go for lunch. He glanced over at her as he turned the truck out of her driveway and immediately burst out laughing.

"Don't you think you're holding onto those a bit too tight?"

She'd been clutching the manilla envelope to her chest like it was life or death. Well, it very nearly had been, but they were safe for now.

"Don't laugh at me!" she turned to him, pleasantly annoyed. "No way are these leaving my hands for even a second until the lawyer takes them, after everything you went through."

"Better close your window," he joked. "Just in case a strong breeze rips them from your grasp."

"Very funny," her bright green eyes widened. "There's no wind, and you're not driving *that* fast."

Their light-hearted banter continued until he pulled into James Garrett's parking lot. Although there was no one menacing in sight, Sawyer waited patiently and watched her until she safely walked through the small building's front doors. He thought of her the entire time he ran errands and picked up supplies. He was so proud of her. She was finally taking complete charge of her life. She texted just before he started driving to his last errand, the lumber store.

"What's he like?" Sawyer asked as she climbed back into the passenger seat.

"Very nice and remarkably meticulous and circumspect. Just what I need."

He noticed she still clutched the manilla envelope.

"He isn't holding onto your paperwork?"

"These are copies. He kept the originals. We have to go to the bank right now so I can get a safety deposit box."

Before heading to the lumber store, they finished that errand, then ran her only other one – a quick trip to the pharmacy where she grabbed some toiletries. Still, Piper leaned against the customer service desk in a great mood as she waited for Sawyer to return from the yard. Noticing a happy young couple browsing one of the aisles, she smiled cheerily at their baby in the stroller. She looked to be about six months old. It wasn't until her mind wandered to her own failed pregnancy attempts and subsequent disloyalty of her husband that her spirits plummeted.

She'd already lost one man, a good man, she'd actually thought at the time, due to her inability to bear children. Would this be the blue-print of her life? When she realized she was thinking of Sawyer and how *he* would feel about a partner that couldn't have kids, she felt twice as uncomfortable and disheartened as before. Stop it, she chided herself. She and Sawyer were just good friends. It would be a waste of her time and futile energy to wish for more, especially in her barren state. He's already been married, she reminded herself, and they were probably planning on a big family...

"Piper, what's wrong?"

She was startled at the sound of his voice. Deep in thought, she hadn't noticed his return.

"Nothing. Just tired, I guess," Piper lied.

Although she did her best to hide her dampened mood throughout lunch, she did an extremely lousy job.

"Well, if you don't want to talk about what's bothering you," Sawyer said before taking another bite of his burger, "I'll just stop asking you."

"There's nothing to ask about," she lied again, for about the fifth time.

She knew his persistent prodding wasn't due to inappropriate nosi-ness or just idle curiosity. It resulted from genuine concern for a friend, so she buried her irritation and smiled at him instead. He really is a fantastic guy, she told herself. An incredible catch for the right woman. If only things were different, the intrusive thought crept in, she'd be the right woman herself.

"You've barely eaten anything. You sure you're done?" Sawyer eyed her confusedly when she finally threw her crumpled napkin onto her plate.

"Too big a breakfast, I guess," another lie, but at least it ended that part of their conversation, and she was able to change its track.

She asked numerous questions about the lumber he'd just picked up. Why this type of wood was preferable for construction? How long would it take them to finish rebuilding the barn, including the roof, before being ready for stalls? If Sawyer knew why she'd suddenly become so interested in all the minute details, he didn't let on. He laboriously answered all her questions until she could think of no more. By that time, they were pulling into her driveway, and she couldn't get out of the passenger seat fast enough.

"Thanks. See you later!" she called over her shoulder as she strode briskly to the house.

Hesitating for a moment with his hand on the truck's door, Sawyer thought of running after her, stopping her and demanding to know what was wrong. But I can't, he grumbled. We're just friends, and that would be more than inappropriate on my part. He morosely threw the truck in reverse, turned right, and headed to the barn to get help and unload.

Thirty-Three

SAWYER WENT to the house later that day, earlier than usual, to help Piper prepare dinner for the men. He was shocked to see the table already neatly set. A huge pot of vegetables was boiling on the stove. When he peered into the oven, he saw a large casserole dish of Shepherd's Pie baking and nearly done. She'd thrown herself into her work, not just to abolish her unpleasant thoughts, but also to avoid spending time with him preparing dinner. She was nowhere in sight, which was odd and somewhat dangerous, since the stovetop and oven were both on. He decided to search for her, using safety as a good excuse.

He nearly ran her down as she entered the kitchen from the living room.

"Well, there you are," he exclaimed, smiling. "I was wondering where you disappeared to with dinner on the go."

"I didn't disappear," she sounded irritated. She'd had much more time to think and become bitter. "I just left for a second to use the restroom, if that's okay with you!"

"Whoa," he lifted his hands in mock surrender. "I wasn't accusing you of anything."

She brushed by him to go and stir the vegetables as if he wasn't there at all. The air in the room was thick with tension, and he knew better, after their afternoon errands, to even attempt to ask her what was wrong.

"Well, it looks like you've got everything under control and don't need my help with supper tonight."

She glanced at him curtly without nodding, so he shuffled defeatedly from the room to continue working in the barn. None of the men seemed to care later, during supper, that Piper wasn't there to eat with them. Sawyer thought they probably just assumed she's busy with something else if they even noticed. Or busy *thinking about something else*, Sawyer mused. When she didn't arrive when dinner concluded, and the men left, he stood and started clearing the dishes. On a whim, he put aside a full plate of Shepherd's Pie and vegetables for her, placing it in the fridge along with a large bowl of salad. Now all she had to do was warm things up.

More than once, he thought of going upstairs to ask her if she was all right, or at least texting her, but he talked himself out of it. For whatever reason, she didn't want to share what was troubling her, and he had no right to push it. We're just friends, he once again reminded himself, reluctantly. All the while wishing that they were much more. If she had similar thoughts despite what was bothering her, and he doubted it, he received no indication as the days wore on. In fact, as the days slowly pushed themselves into next week, he barely saw Piper at all.

She'd gotten very good at cleverly avoiding him. When she realized he was coming into the kitchen earlier and earlier to try and catch her and help her make breakfast, she simply prepared much of it the night before, once he'd already retreated to his room for the night. How she made sure everything tasted fresh and recently prepared was beyond him, but of course, he didn't ask. When he had no choice but to call or text her to discuss the renovations or request her opinion on things, she always made sure to meet him outside to chat when the other men were also around. It became a ridiculous, slow-moving game of tag. For the life of him, Sawyer could never actually catch her and hold her within his space for long.

Not that Piper was pleased with her victory. Inwardly, she was as miserable as she looked. On the few occasions when she forced honesty with herself, she admitted that avoiding Sawyer or hurting him were absolutely the very last things she wanted to do. Not only was she incredibly grateful for everything he'd already done for her, she actually missed him. She longed for his refreshing sense of humor, his comforting presence, and gentle calm. *Why bother?* There was no sense encouraging any sort of long-lasting relationship that would only end in despair. She didn't want to torture herself, or Sawyer, in the long run.

One afternoon, when awakening from her afternoon nap – a new routine that she didn't like at all – she heard the sound of Sawyer's voice through her open window as he said goodbye to the men. Leaping from bed and rushing to look, she saw him get into his vehicle and drive off with what looked like a suitcase. Her heart pounding, thinking he'd deserted her again, she rushed down the stairs and ran straight to the barn.

"Ms. Baker! What's wrong?" Tim asked her.

She realized she looked as panicked and disheveled as she felt. Attempting to catch her breath and compose herself while looking normal, she paused a few moments before answering.

"Everything's fine, Tim. I'm just in a hurry. Do you know where Sawyer went? I need to talk to him about our plans for the stalls."

"Oh, I reckon he'll be back in not too long. Joe's starting his vacation today and has to board his bus soon. Guess his suitcase handle clean came off. Sawyer's making him one of his."

If Tim noticed how awkwardly Piper exhaled after realizing she'd been holding her breath, he kept it to himself.

"I see. All right then. I'll just catch up with Sawyer when he returns, once I have a chance."

Literally heating from the uncomfortable, embarrassing blush in her cheeks, Piper gave him her best casual smile, turned on her heel, and walked as steadily as she could back to the house. She kept her composure all the way through the kitchen, across the living room, and up the stairs until she staggered into her bedroom to collapse, sobbing on her bed. What the hell is wrong with me? She agonized a few minutes later after wiping her tears and sitting up. I'm acting like a ridiculous, clingy, lovesick schoolgirl. Or like one of those needy heroines in those ill-fated romances she'd loved to read growing up.

Well, I'm grown up now, she huffed, grabbing a tissue from the container on her nightstand, and stood up. Silly stories aren't my thing anymore, she reminded herself. And neither are futile wishes and hopeless dreams. After blowing her nose and combing her tousled hair, she went downstairs to make a large, comforting mug of hot chocolate. It wasn't until she'd seated herself at the kitchen table that she remembered the last time she'd so needed one.

It's a mighty warm night for you to be enjoying such a hot drink. Sawyer's words, and his forced absence, haunted her. She took a slow sip and stared down at the steam rising from her mug. She pushed it further away from her on the table. Hot chocolate may have worked when she was a child, but it sure as heck wasn't doing anything for her now.

Thirty-Four

PIPER CONTINUED AVOIDING HIM, despite her scare of thinking that Sawyer was leaving again. She convinced herself that it didn't matter in the long run, and if he left, so be it. She'd just have to suck it up. She told herself, I might as well get used to not having him around because he sure won't be around forever. Once the renovations were complete, as her employee, he was free to leave. And what makes me think, she continually wondered, that he even wants a romantic relationship with me. She'd already told him about her husband's cheating and divorcing her due to her inability to have children. She was sure that this fact would have extinguished his amorous intentions, if he'd had any in the first place. Now I just have to get used to it, she prodded herself.

That quest became more difficult as the days passed. It turned out she couldn't avoid Sawyer's presence for as long as she thought. A few days later, up late and eating dinner alone in the dining room, she was startled to see Sawyer, still dressed in his work clothes, come waltzing in.

"I've been waiting for you to have a chance to talk to me. Tim mentioned you wanted to discuss our plans for the cattle stalls."

He gazed at her as if her eating dinner this close to bedtime was the most normal thing in the world. As if he didn't realize she'd done it this long to avoid dining with him and the other men. Well, really to avoid dining or spending any time with *him*. She stammered for words for a moment, feeling as if she was suddenly enveloped by fog. She hadn't expected to be alone with him, and worse, she hadn't expected it to still feel so good.

"Yes," she finally found her voice. "But we can talk about it in the morning. I'll meet you in the barn once you guys get to work."

"Or we can discuss it now," he smirked, pulling up a chair and sliding close to her.

Bastard, she thought, but could not thwart the smile creeping up on her face. Discuss the stalls calmly, she told herself. Don't veer off topic and get into anything other than your renovation plans. *The last thing I want to do is embarrass myself by admitting why I've been avoiding him or how I feel, because his feelings for me cannot be the same, at least not long term.*

"Free stalls? Isn't that what we were thinking before?" he asked.

She realized she couldn't quite remember what free stalls were in her muddled thoughts.

"I think so," she said. "Just remind me what free stalls are again."

Unperturbed, he slowly explained their setup. When in the barn, the cattle would be free to come and go as they pleased and to walk into individual, three-sided bedding areas whenever they wished to lie down. He reminded her that this was preferable to other housing methods because it kept the cattle clean and dry.

"They can't soil their beds," he said, "because there isn't enough room for them to turn around. They have to stand up and back out. This will also save us big time on bedding costs because there will be far less bedding used in the long run."

"Right," she nodded, recalling what they'd previously discussed and noticing, with a skip of her heart, that he used the word *us*.

Stop it, she chided herself. You're reading too much into it. Sawyer is your ranch manager, a part of your working ranch, and that's all he means.

"So, what was it you wanted to discuss exactly?"

Was it her imagination? Did he just lean slightly closer to her?

"Tim said you wanted to discuss the stalls. Did you just want clarification of what we'd basically already decided to do? A quick reminder of what free stalls are?"

Annoyed at herself for looking like a deer in headlights for a moment, she nodded yes.

"I just wanted to make sure our plans for everything were still on track," she finally said.

"Okay, good."

He smiled at her but didn't get up from the table. They looked at each other awkwardly for a moment, then looked away. Why doesn't he just go? Piper agonized, struggling to keep a composed look on her face. Sawyer, on the other hand, looked calm and relaxed. Inwardly, however, he was also a bundle of nerves. Piper's strange behavior since their errands in town had thoroughly shaken and confused him.

What's more, his great concern over her seeming depression unnerved him. But he didn't let her know that. For whatever reason, she'd chosen not to share her feelings for him, and he had to respect that. But, he eyed her affectionately, that didn't mean he had to go anywhere.

After a few minutes of awkward silence, Piper started picking at her meal with her fork. She had to do something, and all she could think of was to eat. Her frazzled nerves had reduced her appetite, and it became more and more difficult to swallow with every bite. Damn him, she thought. Why on earth is he just sitting here? She was about to say something when he finally spoke first.

"I'm not going to ask you what's wrong again. I've done that a million times already, and I respect your wishes not to tell me, or even be in the same room with me, it seems. What I will do is simply tell you that if ever you need to talk, I'm here."

With that, he pushed his chair back and stood. Neither of them wanted him to leave. When Piper still didn't say anything, he turned away and began walking from the room.

"Sawyer?" her voice was shaky and thin.

Whatever's eating at her must be horrible, he thought. He turned to look at her and was dismayed by the pain in her face.

"Is it anything I've said or done?" he asked.

"No! Of course not," she answered quickly. "I just seem to be at a crossroads of sorts within myself. I mean, as far as what I want for my future and with making realistic plans."

"Piper, you're capable of anything!" he walked back to the table and leaned down towards her. "Just think of everything you've been faced with, what you've already been through and how far you've come!"

At least he still believes in me, she thought with a smile. If nothing else, at least that hasn't changed. However, looking into his intent eyes, she wished she could tell him that she wanted so much more. Instead, she forced a pleasant laugh.

"Are you going to call me brave again?"

"If I have to," he chuckled, smiling back.

He sat back down, and they talked about everything except what was indeed on their minds. But at least they were talking again and joking and laughing. It's a start, Sawyer acknowledged gratefully, as she inwardly celebrated the very same thing.

Thirty-Five

PIPER WATCHED the backhoe scoop another huge load of dirt and dump it to the side, as the machine slowly made its way to the barn. Sawyer had discovered numerous problems with the water lines leading to the building and thought it best for her to replace them. As he'd explained, sure, she could simply repair them, but it was a job she'd have to do over and over again. And that would be neither pleasant nor easy if it ever had to be done in the winter when the thirsty cattle were already there. He'd said that the underground piping was ancient and hadn't weathered the years very well by the looks of things. The men were already working with the plumber, who'd arrived just after dawn, on replacing and rerouting the water pipes inside the barn.

She scanned the area, looking for Sawyer. She saw him just inside the building, looking at sketches from the electrician. Things were coming along nicely. Piper was actually surprised at how quickly the renovations had progressed. Sawyer had told her that the roofers were scheduled to come in a few weeks. She hadn't understood exactly why she needed them since the men had already finished the mainframe and sides of the barn, including the roof.

"We've only used wood," he had explained. "That will eventually rot if it's not covered with metal and metal roofing is not my expertise."

She had laughed and approved his calling professional barn roofers, realizing she'd somehow thought, up to that point, that Sawyer was good at everything. He looked away from the paperwork and noticed her standing there. Gesturing for her to wait for him and not run off, he quickly finished his conversation and jogged up to her.

"Leaving already?"

"Yup. Thought I'd get an early start."

He nodded, rejoicing at how happy and adventurous she looked again. Their little chat had, thank God, somehow rejuvenated her. And whether or not he could take all the credit, he was just glad to see Piper back to her old self. She'd actually written long lists of renovation plans for the house once he was finished with the barn. Even though it would be a while before he could get to it, she'd decided to do a little bit of decorating in advance. She was going into town to buy some paintings and perhaps some other types of art.

"You can start out at Wallack's near the corner of Maple and Chester. Maybe have a quick look at the flea market, that'll be open this afternoon too. But I'm sure you'll find something you like at Esteria Treasures. It's been open forever, and people come to it from miles around."

"Okay," she smirked, "But if I buy any big, heavy items, guess who's helping me carry them into the house?"

Piper's good mood lasted all through her drive to town. Things were normal again. She was feeling normal again. No matter what the future held in store, or didn't, for the both of them, they would just take it one day, one step at a time. Worry doesn't become you, her mother had told her frequently when she was a child., and even when she hit high school, and the ever-present teen angst had clouded her face. Deep in thought with happy memories of growing up, she nearly drove by the flea market until she realized it was already open. She decided to stop there first.

Held inside a large wooden building with huge sliding doors open to let in the fresh, warm summer air. Why hadn't I thought of coming here before? She smiled. Making her way along the adjoining tables, she examined much of their contents before strolling over to the vendors' booths against the walls. If she would've had a shopping addiction, she'd have already filled the back of her pickup before returning to purchase more.

The market had a much more extensive selection than she'd imagined. Figurines, woven baskets, hand-carved wooden statues, posters, pictures, dishes, tablecloths, linen and blankets, clothing of every sort. Shaken for a moment when she walked up to a booth displaying children's clothes and toys, she smiled pleasantly at the amiable woman seated behind the table and simply walked casually on. Nope, her inner voice spoke loud and clear. No way will I let any unpleasant thoughts creep into my mind today. Before leaving, she purchased some handmade wreaths to hang near the fireplace, some warm quilts for her bed this winter, and a very large and ornamental birdhouse that she'd get Sawyer to hang outside her kitchen's large picture window. She rushed back to a booth and bought some wild birdseed as a quick afterthought.

Wallack's was next, but she didn't find much of anything she liked there. Although the young girl behind the counter was super friendly and helpful, she left with only a large tote bag picturing Appaloosa horses running through lush green fields. As it turned out, Sawyer was right about her last stop, Esteria Treasures, being the best. She loved the shop as soon as she'd set foot in the door. It was loaded with curios and fantastic artwork, mostly high-quality photos and posters, and oil paintings, some large enough to take up entire walls. The place even had that old-world, artistic, comforting smell that made you feel right at home. She'd been browsing for over half an hour and was finally trying to decide between two oil paintings when Sawyer walked in.

"Though I'd find you here," he smiled. "Had to go to Becker's Hardware for some last-minute items and figured I'd track you down. Find anything you like?"

"Did you see the back of my truck when you walked in?" she laughed. "I can't decide now between these two oil paintings. What do you think?"

The elderly clerk had removed the large pieces from the walls and displayed them on easels side by side to help make her choice. The one on the left depicted the living room of an old farmstead. A contented beagle curled up, sleeping in front of the roaring fireplace. It was quaint and charming and filled with exquisite detail right up to the frayed ends of the quilt that hung over the wooden rocking chair. The painting to the right was of three gorgeous and majestic horses – Percherons, the clerk told her – standing strong and free in the pasture with manes blowing briskly in the wind. The two in the forefront were obviously mare and foal. Their white-speckled dark gray coats and golden manes glistened in the sun. A little ways behind them, the stallion was a much darker, deeper gray.

"Wow," Sawyer exclaimed. "They're both fantastic." Then, looking at the prices written on the tiny tags held to the corners of the frames by delicate strings, he shook his head. "I don't want to recommend either and have you mad at me when you wish you'd bought the one you left behind."

They stood there talking it over, deciding where each would look best hanging in her house, for quite a while. The conversation veered to her one day getting her own herd of horses and, before that, her very own dog. It seemed right talking about all of it – the art to complement her house, her future animals – with Sawyer. He was a part of it all. She felt it, and he felt it too, or so they both hoped. Finally, she called to the clerk, Gerald, at the counter.

"I'll take them both," she said.

"Piper, are you sure?" Sawyer grabbed at her arm. "Did you look at the prices? They're both in the high three figures."

"I know," she smiled. "But they're both beautiful and feel like home."

So do you, he thought silently but merely smiled. As they drove home separately, their thoughts raced along similar paths. Their collaborative art purchase felt right. Their collaboration was nothing official, but it felt secure.

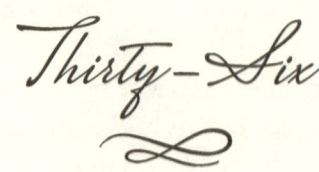

Thirty-Six

SAWYER HAD JUST GONE BACK OUTSIDE to the barn after helping Piper carry her purchases into the house when her cell phone rang. She quickly fished it from her purse to avoid losing the call.

"Mom!" she said excitedly. "I haven't heard from you or dad in a while."

"And we could say the same for you," her mother sounded stern, although it was very apparent she was so happy to talk to her.

"I'm sorry," Piper sighed. "I've just been so busy here with renovations. The barn is almost restored."

She hadn't told her parents about the fire, the robbery, or about almost getting shot. As far as they knew, the barn just had to be rebuilt from scratch because it had been in such bad shape.

"Got pictures?" her mom asked hopefully. "You haven't sent us anything for weeks."

"I'll take some today," she promised before telling her mother all about the oil paintings and the rest of her shopping trip.

While her mother listened intently, and Piper could tell she was truly engaged, she suddenly got the weird feeling that something wasn't quite right. Something a little edgy darkened her mom's typically cheery voice.

"What's wrong?" she asked her outright. "I know that tone."

"Well," she hesitated for a second, "I just thought I'd better call you in case you hadn't already heard. John is getting married to *that* woman. She's very pregnant with his child."

"Oh," Piper gasped, feeling as if the wind had been knocked out of her. "I see."

"I'm so sorry, Piper. I know how difficult it must...."

"Mom, I'm fine! Trust me, I have no love for John. I'm just a little surprised, is all, that he's getting remarried so quickly. We haven't even finalized our divorce."

"Well," her mother sneered, "with one in the oven...."

"Ugh, don't remind me about how angry I am over that!"

"Sorry. Let's change the subject, dear. What else is new with you?"

They chatted pleasantly for about a half-hour before Piper excused herself. It was time to begin making supper for the men, and she still had to put all her purchases away. Sawyer had promised to hang her paintings right after dinner was done. Her new house would soon feel even more like her home.

She was carrying her folded quilts upstairs to her bedroom when she suddenly remembered what she had in her closet beside her bed. Definitely, some things she didn't want marring her new home's fresh and joyful atmosphere. Out with the old, in with the new, she smirked as she pulled the boxes of old photographs out of her closet. She found the albums filled with family pictures with John, before and after they were married, and her wedding photographs.

"You're headed upstairs to the attic, as soon as Sawyer can get you up the ladder and into the dust," she exclaimed.

It felt delicious to turn the page on that painful chapter of her life.

Thirty-Seven

PIPER SETTLED on a simple meal for everyone because she was running a little late after putting everything away. One that they'd enjoy. She was forming the last of the hamburger patties when Sawyer walked in.

"Can you make the bacon and cut the cheese?" she looked at him hopefully. "I've already made the potato salad. It's cooling in the fridge."

"Sure thing," he said happily. "You decide yet where you want the paintings hung?"

"Almost. I could use your input. I've never had such gorgeous paintings before."

"Really?" he seemed surprised.

She hadn't told him much about her parents' home or her married life. Still, he'd definitely gotten the impression that her parents and her husband were very well off. And people with lots of money usually splurge on fine art.

"Yeah. My mom's taste in artwork is kind of abstract. Really not my thing. I don't really know what dad likes; he just goes along with mom," she laughed. "When I was married, our house was filled with futuristic art. Not my thing. It was John's."

"Ah, so you never really had a home filled with expressions of yourself."

"Why, Sawyer, that's so on point! I never really thought of it like that."

She loved the profound, straightforward way he saw things for exactly what they were. It was a talent she hadn't quite mastered yet, but one she hoped to perfect as time went on. As she carried the plates of burgers outside to the large barbeque, she realized how much she loved just about everything about Sawyer. His sense of honor, honesty, integrity, sense of humor, and of course, his rugged good looks. She was actually blushing, thinking about it, when he slid up to her side.

"Here are the buns. We'll toast them lightly too."

Dinner was a delicious and happy one. Piper sat right among the men, laughing and joking right along with them, all the while her mind centering on how she'd been so lucky to build such a happy new home. She rushed Sawyer through the dishes because she could hardly wait to get her paintings hung.

"I'll finish putting them all in the rack," he insisted. "Go wander around the house and try to decide where each piece would look the best."

A few minutes later, he found her still wandering from room to room, looking perplexed.

"I love each painting so much that I can't decide where to give each equal space and equal opportunities for view."

"Hmmm," he cocked his head as he looked around. "Where do you spend most of your time?"

"In the kitchen, living room, and bedroom."

"Kitchen's out," he snickered, "so maybe living room and bedroom it is then."

He waited patiently while she pondered the monumental decision of which piece went into each of the two rooms. Finally, she decided the painting with the beagle should go above the fireplace because it depicted a fireplace scene. The beautiful horses would hang on the wall across from the foot of her bed, so she'd wake up seeing them all the time.

"Let's relax and have a beer first," she suggested, "before I make you lug those heavy paintings around again."

"Won't argue with that. I'll grab them," he said, heading to the kitchen.

"Did you have art in your house, I mean when you were married?" she asked a few minutes later after they'd settled comfortably on the couch.

"Yup, but nothing super expensive or elaborate. Just some nice large, framed photos and posters we purchased at auctions and second-hand stores. Peggy-Lee loved shopping at those."

"What was she like?" she asked him, realizing she had not a spec of jealousy. Instead, she felt incredibly sorry for the woman who had not only lost her life but, in doing so, also the best man alive.

"Beautiful, ambitious, talented, and driven. With a wicked sense of humor. She never failed to make me laugh. Even when we shouldn't have been laughing. She had a talent for that."

"Did you guys want kids?"

"Yeah. We were just planning to start a family when..." his voice trailed off as his memories caught up.

"Oh, Sawyer, I'm sorry. I didn't mean to pry or to bring this up. I always say the stupidest things."

"No, Piper, you don't," he looked at her evenly. "You're just very innocent and forthright."

"Hah!" she cut him off. "I'm not so sure those are great attributes to have."

"I like them," he smiled.

They ended up talking about their exes and how they each dealt with the loss. She told Sawyer about her mother's call informing her that John was soon to wed his very pregnant girlfriend. Nestled so close to Sawyer on the couch, she realized it didn't bother her one bit. She told him that the only thing she regretted was that she'd wasted so much time in her marriage once it went wrong.

Nodding his understanding, Sawyer opened up to her about his own regrets and guilt. About how, for a long time, he'd felt responsible for his wife's death. Blamed himself for not preventing it, for not being home when she was attacked.

"It's not your fault, Sawyer," Piper said earnestly, patting his shoulder.

"I know that *now*. I just didn't for a very long time."

Soon, their conversation drifted to happier things. How good the ranch was looking, what great plans they had to build it up once the livestock arrived. And even how fantastic it was for them to be able to talk freely and openly to one another. How glad they both were to be friends. Finally, Sawyer announced he'd better hang the paintings before he got too tired. He had to be up early again and outside when the plumber and electrician came back.

He'd finished hanging the horses in her room and was about to go back downstairs when she noticed the boxes of photographs still on her bed.

"Wait. Please, carry these up to the attic for me? I'll never make it up that rickety ladder."

"What are these? All photos?"

"Yes. Chapters of my life I want to close."

He looked at her sympathetically for a moment, then grabbed the first box. The photo album on top slid off and fell open onto the bed. He picked it up to put it back, and a photo caught his eye. Piper, and a bunch of other people, posing at the beach. His heart jumped as he took a closer look.

"Who's that?" his finger pointed at the man beside her.

"That's John, my ex-husband."

"Piper," his eyes widened, "that's the man I saw in the cottage. The one I didn't recognize with Noah and Job."

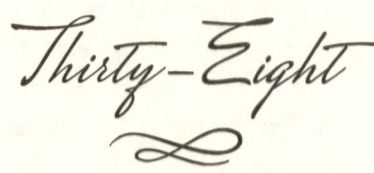

Thirty-Eight

"THAT'S IMPOSSIBLE!" Piper shook her head and gazed at Sawyer in disbelief.

He has to be mistaken, she thought. Whoever he actually saw must just look a lot like John. There was no other plausible explanation. She tried to explain to Sawyer before he could say another word.

"John hardly ever even mentioned this ranch the entire time we were married. He's never been interested in it, never had any ties to it or to anyone here at all. That's why it fell into such disrepair. There's absolutely no way the man you saw in the cottage was him."

"Piper," Sawyer said very gently, reeling at the anguished look in her eyes, "I know what I saw, *who* I saw. The man in the suit was your ex-husband, John."

She scowled and shook her head again.

"You said yourself, you were crouched down at the window. How well could you have really seen and heard everything? Besides, I'm sure your attention was more focused on Noah and Job."

"It was focused on all three of them," he insisted, "and I saw and heard everything clearly, I'm sure."

"So, what did you hear exactly? Let's go over this again. There's no way that man was my ex-husband!"

He was shocked at the realization but obviously not as appalled as her, so he could remain calm. Putting the photo album back on top of the others in the box, he pushed everything to the far edge of the bed and gestured for Piper to sit down next to him and talk. She hesitated for a moment, in actuality wanting nothing more than to drop the entire topic, sensing that whatever he was about to say wasn't going to be good. Or, at the very least, that it wouldn't definitively rule John out as the man he saw.

"Like I told you before, the man was furious at Noah, saying something about Noah not keeping up his end of the bargain. Later, when I was hidden in the back of Noah's truck, I heard the man tell Noah that he was sick and tired of his promises and excuses."

"Excuses for what?" Piper snapped.

"For not doing and accomplishing whatever he was supposed to, apparently. And Piper, it was very, very obvious the man in the suit wasn't from around here."

That didn't mean anything in and of itself, and Piper told him so.

"Is John in the habit of wearing a suit?" Sawyer eyed her pointedly.

"Well, he's not the only one!"

Sawyer sighed. He wasn't getting anywhere and sensed that if he pushed it further at the moment, Piper would simply get more upset and angry and dig in her heels.

"Let's talk about it later," he stood and grasped the box once again to take it up to the attic.

"No," she groaned, "let's talk about it now."

He put the box back down and sat beside her on the bed.

"I don't know what else to say to you. The man in the picture is the same man I saw in the cottage with Noah and Job."

Piper's head was spinning. She could barely understand her own racing thoughts. She searched her mind for a solution, for any plausible explanation of what was going on. Finally, as Sawyer sat quietly staring at her, she latched onto a possible cause. Maybe the mistaken identity was simply a result of the man in the cottage looking a lot like John in that *one* photograph. She stood, slid the box in front of her, and began frantically leafing through the photo album until she found more pictures of John. More photos of him at the beach that day, some at

Christmas at her parents' place, one or two at his office, and even a few taken of him during his fishing trip with his friends only a few years ago. She pulled them from their sleeves.

"See?" she smirked at Sawyer. "John doesn't always look like he did in that photo. Look how his hair is a little longer here...."

"It's the same man," he cut her off. "I'm so sorry."

"Sorry?!" her retort verged on a scream. "The only thing you should be sorry for is your misidentification based on an obstructed view of a conversation you had little time to see and hear."

Arguing with her was pointless, and besides, it was the last thing he wanted to do. He stood again.

"Do you still want me to take the box of photos to the attic?"

"Whatever...sure," she huffed.

Left to her own confused and frazzled thoughts when he was out of the room, Piper went over everything, trying to sort and quiet the whirling thoughts in her mind. Sawyer *could* actually be mistaken. John wasn't the only man who favored suits. Besides, she consoled herself, lots of people in this world look alike, especially businessmen in office attire. Men in suits, she grunted, had a certain look. And, examining her own situation closely, sure, she and John were divorcing, but he had loved her once. Why would he suddenly be working against her now? Especially when he had been the one to offer her the ranch. In a quick bid to hasten our settlement and get rid of me, she cringed. Even so, why would he want to complicate the divorce and take it away from her now? It didn't make any sense.

By the time Sawyer came back downstairs to her bedroom, she'd once again cemented her thought that it couldn't have been John he saw.

"Well, I'd better get going," he said quietly. "I have to be up and outside by six when the electrician and plumber return."

Maybe he's just jealous of John, Piper mused. For some insane reason, she just couldn't let it go. After all, she thought, I was married to John for a long time. And he is very wealthy and successful. In many ways, he's everything that Sawyer is not. With common sense and rationality out the window, due to her wounded pride and self-worth, she goaded Sawyer into a pointless argument. Even though, deep down, she knew it was a very good thing that Sawyer was everything that John was not.

"Fine, go then," she snipped, "if you'd rather not face up to the fact that you're wrong. John has his faults, quite obviously, but he's not the evil, vicious man you're trying to make him out to be."

Knowing he should just leave before things truly exploded, Sawyer couldn't resist attempting to salvage his honor in the face of her disrespect.

"I'm not trying to make John out to be anything that he isn't. I'm simply telling you that he was in the cottage with Noah and Job that day."

Although it was totally irrational, his vehement insistence felt like another attack on her. As if he's claiming that John was somehow mixed up with Noah and victimizing her, amplified her victimization all the more. Especially when Sawyer *could* be wrong.

"We're done discussing this," she sneered. "In fact, I'm through with talking to you at all."

Thirty-Nine

PIPER STOOD SLOWLY to get ready for bed, sitting tensely on the bed until she heard the door shut, as he entered the ranch hands' quarters that were within her house. First, she went downstairs to shut all the lights off. Glancing at the fireside painting that Sawyer had just hung in her living room, she felt such a stab of despair that she actually moaned out loud. So much for my fantastic, reliable, and safe friendship with Sawyer, she sighed, and my efforts here to create a peaceful and happy home. She shuffled to the kitchen and considered making a hot chocolate before quickly clicking off the lights. Not like *that* had worked lately either. Feeling like a total lost cause and failure, she ambled upstairs to her room.

To be confronted by the second painting of the peaceful, gentle horses looking back at her from their placid field. Ugh, why did everything she touch seem to crumble beneath her? Every wish, every dream, every hope for a new and joyful life. Desperately trying to allay her racing thoughts, she splashed cold water on her face in her adjoining bathroom. She resigned herself to her mind's frenzied journey. Maybe, just maybe, she could sort things out and regain a handle on things. After about a half-hour, she realized it wasn't going to happen. She was just too upset to think straight about anything.

Before her horrible dreams took over, the last thing she remembered was gazing at the horses in the painting, hoping for some peace and serenity. They looked calm and content but, instead of endowing her with tranquility, she actually felt like they were mocking her. She felt as though everyone and everything around her was as happy as she was not. She tossed and turned fitfully until morning, often awakening from terrible dreams. She was a child again, locked out of her parent's house while they ignored her frantic banging at the door and her screams. Then, a bride at her wonderfully extravagant wedding, but the groom beside her at the altar didn't exist.

She awoke in the morning in a cold sweat. Glancing at the alarm clock on her nightstand, she was shocked to see it was already a quarter past eight. Much too late to begin making breakfast for the men. She struggled up on her elbows to listen. They were laughing and joking down in the kitchen. Sawyer must have stepped in and made them something to eat. Just the thought of food nauseated her, so she decided to remain upstairs in her room until breakfast was over and, hopefully, Sawyer cleaned the remaining food and dishes up. Once she'd strained her ears to nothing but silence for more than fifteen minutes, she made her way downstairs.

She couldn't stomach coffee, but a nice cold glass of orange juice would be nice. The kitchen was empty, cleaned, and welcoming, and she poured herself a glass. Get ahold of yourself, she chided, as she pulled the belt of her robe tighter and sat down at the table. Thoughts of John, and Sawyer's steadfast insistence he'd been the man in the cottage, flooded her mind. Stop it, she actually said out loud. That discussion was over. Ended. Topic closed. Let Sawyer believe what he wanted. She wasn't going to concern herself with dismal *possibilities*. From here on in, she would focus only on proven facts.

"Ms. Baker?" Tim peeked his head inside the kitchen door.

She startled but quickly regained her composure, at least as much as she could.

"Good morning, Tim. What's up?"

"Sawyer's busy with the electrician. He asked me to get a fresh pot of coffee going on the machine for you because he forgot when he went outside. By the way, he saved a big plate of bacon and eggs for you. It's in the fridge. I hope you're feeling better now."

"Better?" she recoiled.

What exactly had Sawyer told the men?

"Yes, he told us you were sleeping in because of your cold or flu."

"Oh," she exhaled deeply and couldn't help but smile. "I guess it was just a headache because I feel much better now."

"Great," Tim smiled. "So, would you still like me to put that pot of coffee on, or...."

"No, I can do it myself, thanks. You go on and get back to work. It's fine."

He nodded amiably and shut the door. Still unable to stomach coffee, Piper sat quietly, sipping her orange juice. Vacillating between her love of Sawyer's warm and caring personality and the small amount of loyalty to John that she still possessed. That's it, she slammed her hand down on the table! Somehow, inadvertently, stupidly, she'd felt as if she had Sawyer tugging on one side of her emotions with John pulling at the other. She'd placed herself into a ridiculous, unwarranted situation when it wasn't up to her to make a choice. Sawyer was her friend. John was her ex-husband. Whether it was truly him in the cottage or not – and she was still extremely hesitant to believe it – it had nothing to do with Sawyer's actions and feelings towards her. She was still very angry at him for not considering that he might be wrong about what he saw.

She considered calling John to get to the bottom of it. She'd actually pulled her cell from her robe's pocket before she stopped herself. John hadn't been exactly open and honest with her, especially in the last few months of their fading marriage. He was a liar and a cheat. Would he actually tell her the truth if it was really him in the cottage? Likely not, she answered her own question and laid her cell down on the table. Time would tell whether she or Sawyer was right. Until then, or at least until Sawyer admitted to the possibility that he could be wrong, she resolved to keep a healthy distance from him. There was no sense in complicating her already chaotic and problematic life.

Just as she had before, she masterfully avoided spending time with Sawyer. She prepared much of each day's breakfast the night before, after Sawyer had retired to the ranch hands' quarters, so she didn't have to prepare it with him in the morning. She cooked each evening's dinner alone, preparing it by mid-afternoon at the latest when Sawyer was still outside working with his crew. After showing up a few times an hour or so before supper break to help her cook, Sawyer quickly clued in that, once again, she'd decided that she didn't need him anymore. This was enough to fuel his own anger. He couldn't believe how quickly she dismissed his explicit assertions based on facts in favor of some strange sense of loyalty to the man who'd so cruelly dumped her and let her down.

Tension was high between them, and often, he now avoided her too when he could. They mainly spoke via quick hand-written notes placed on the fridge or kitchen table and by texts, only meeting face to face when they had no other choice. Even so, the longer it went on, the more it saddened and angered him. The final straw was when she came out to the barn one day, deliberately ignoring his presence, and asked Tim for an update on the plumber's and electrician's work. Not that Tim didn't know the basic facts. But that's my job and responsibility, Sawyer fumed that day, and she's intentionally brushing me aside. He told himself that all he had to do was declare to her that he just *might* be wrong about what he saw, even though he was one hundred percent certain he wasn't. His sense of pride and honor wouldn't allow it. Not even if it meant he and Piper eventually severing ties.

My days here at Piper's side are numbered, he thought, and he wasn't totally wrong.

Forty

"YOU GOING to replace those bricks around the fireplace?" Tim asked Sawyer as he walked past it, carrying more supplies inside with Jason, another ranch hand on their crew.

"Nah, not right now anyway," Sawyer answered. "No real rush on that."

He had decided to renovate the small ranch hand's cottage on Piper's property, on the other side of the driveway from her house. It had once served as private quarters for the ranch manager, and he figured that it was the best place for him to stay with things so cold and tense between him and Piper. Colder weather was still far off, so no, he didn't need the fireplace yet. And, he sighed as he watched the men leave to go and grab more lumber. The truth of the matter was that he really doubted, the way things were going, that he'd still be here by the time that winter hit.

Piper had ramped up her efforts to avoid him, so he hadn't even bothered to clear his renovation of the cottage with her. He doubted she'd mind, primarily because he worked on it in his spare time, not when he was working to collect his paycheck from her. He'd actually considered using his own money for the repairs but then decided against it. The cottage was his only while he remained employed by her. His repairs and upgrades would simply increase her property value, and she was free to offer it to whomever she hired one day to take his place.

"Anything else you want to be brought in?" Tim asked, setting the large pails filled with nails and screws down on the wood floor.

"No, that's it, thanks. I'll have everything I need to get back to work on it later tonight. Let's go and see what the electrician's cleared for us to do. If the wiring's done in the back half of the barn, we can begin putting up the new wood panels for the backs of the stalls."

Taking a last look around as they filed outside, Sawyer was shaken by the depths of his despair. Until that very moment, he hadn't fully absorbed how much it hurt him to be moving out of Piper's house. Moving out of her life, in essence. At least as a friend. He was now simply her ranch manager, like it or not.

"Sawyer!" Will waved at him as he neared the barn. "Piper was just here looking for you."

His heart rattled and jumped in his chest, despite his efforts to remain aloof and stoic. He chided himself. Like a lovesick teenage boy, he jolted at just the mention of her name. And she was looking for him. Maybe she'd finally decided to let the issue of her ex-husband in the cottage disintegrate. Knowing Piper's strong will and determination, that wasn't likely, but he could always hope. Nodding a quick thank you to Will, he made his way across the grass to the farmhouse.

Piper was outside sweeping the porch.

"You were looking for me?" he asked, careful to keep his voice neutral and calm.

"Yes," she looked up and gazed at him without, of course, the long-absent smile on her face.

At least she didn't just text or write me a note, Sawyer mused silently as he braced himself. Her wishing to speak with him face to face was either exceptionally bad or extraordinarily good. Or so he thought. As it turned out, it was neither. Just simple confirmation of where they stood.

"I've just noticed that you're renovating the cottage," her tone had an icy edge.

"On my own time," he quickly jumped in, "not while under your paycheck. The supplies are yours, but the reno will add value to...."

"That's not what I'm getting at," she quipped. "You didn't think it was a good idea to speak to me about it first? You're the *ranch manager*," the words cut through him like a knife, "but still, everything that's done here has to go through me."

She was his boss, no longer his friend, and she'd just made that abundantly clear. She was stirred up enough about it to not just simply shoot him a text.

"My apologies," he said in his best all-business voice. "I'll make sure to clear everything with you from now on. But Piper," he hesitated, "with things so strained between us, I honestly didn't think you'd mind seeing a little less of me once I moved out."

There. He said it. Even though it wasn't all he wanted to say, far from it. What he really longed to do was grab her by the shoulders and shake her. Ask her whether her dogged protection of her ex-husband was really worth destroying the friendship between them. The friendship that had been on the verge of becoming so much more. If she sensed his turmoil, or if she wrestled with her own anxiety, she didn't show it. She simply nodded her understanding of his reasoning.

"Fine. Clear it with me before you decorate if you want to do anything major."

Said as if she hadn't valued his opinion while decorating her own house.

"You got it," he turned abruptly before walking briskly back to the barn.

She looked away but then back again, watching him walk. Only to the barn for the moment, but it felt like he was walking right out of her life. Piper's heart sank as she came to the realization that his move to the cottage likely really *was* the first step of his sauntering out of her life. He now considered himself nothing more than an employee, and once the work on her ranch was done, he would be too. Reeling from the sudden, smothering feelings of abandonment, Piper leaned the broom against the porch railing and went into the house. First John, she pondered, now Sawyer. In the end, the reasons didn't matter. What mattered was she'd been abandoned again.

Sawyer grimly forged his way through the workday, not feeling any better than Piper. He had more than a little trouble concentrating. He went over the electrician's diagrams and final plans before giving him the go-ahead. *Thank God I've already gone over everything with the plumber*, he thought, knowing his distracted thoughts predisposed him to make a mistake. For the remainder of the day, he decided to simply help his crew. *Manual labor is just the thing when I don't want to think anymore.* But it didn't turn out the way he thought.

He found himself thinking about Piper no matter what he did. Nailing wood up for the back stalls, he found himself wondering if Piper's ex-husband even knew how to properly hold let alone swing a hammer and whether Piper had even cared. Her strange loyalty to John unnerved him and, despite his usual confidence, made him wonder what he himself lacked. When finally, it was time for dinner, he actually cringed at the thought of going into the house.

Of course, Piper would already have supper laid out on the table, so she didn't have to be there, but still, her marked absence grated on his soul. None of the men seemed to notice or care when they seated themselves and began piling food onto their plates. Wondering if Piper was even a fraction as miserable as he was, Sawyer did his best to join their conversation, to joke and laugh.

It wasn't until later, as he washed the dishes on his own that he felt the heated waves of anger creep in again. *I haven't done anything to deserve this*, he grunted, *except tell Piper the truth.* He had no idea why it affected her so deeply. What he did know was that, with or without him, she'd better get a rein on her emotions if she wanted to make a success of the ranch and of her life. No matter how much he wanted to help her, no matter how much he missed her and wanted her to trust and enjoy his company again, he could do nothing but watch and wait.

Less than two weeks later, lying wide awake on his bed in the middle of the night after he'd moved into the cottage, the same intrusive thoughts haunted him. Piper needed to work through her issues and overcome her state of denial before they could even hope of getting their relationship back to what it had been.

Forty-One

THAT SAME NIGHT, Piper lay awake in bed for hours before finally sitting up and grabbing her phone. Until now, she'd avoided John's profile on Facebook, and he'd unfriended her anyways – no surprise there! – but she couldn't take her morbid curiosity any longer and decided to have a look. Hopefully, he hadn't made his posts private. If not, she could creep him and maybe get some insight into what, if anything, he had to say about her and their impending divorce. Flustered at how her anxiety tightened her chest, she searched for and found him and clicked on his profile. Seconds later, she was sorry she did.

The tiny photo she'd seen in search results had been hard to make out and see clearly, but now it stared right back up at her from her screen like a painful slap in the face. There she was, the woman that had destroyed her marriage, smiling sweetly, wrapped tightly in John's arms. He had posted their picture to show the world how content and happy he was now. And by the looks of it, if pictures didn't lie, he truly was.

She was much younger than Piper, at least by ten years. Some, Piper cringed, would say she was prettier. It really depended on taste. Either way, Becky had what Piper didn't – the man she had married, the man who'd once vowed his faithfulness and undying love for her. From what her mother had said, she now also had Piper's house, her luxury vehicle, it had been in John's name, so she'd had no choice but to leave it. Worse, or best of all, depending on how you looked at it, she also carried the baby John had wanted from the start. As Piper scrolled with shaking fingers, she learned Becky's last name. Henderson. But it wouldn't be her last name for long.

John's posts were filled with details of their wonderful plans for their elaborate wedding. Piper scowled as she noticed that Becky looked heavier, more and more pregnant as the posts progressed. Well, of course, she sighed. What was I thinking? That the bitch's pregnancy and the illegitimate baby would just evaporate? Not illegitimate for long, she reminded herself as she continued scrolling. They planned to marry before their son was born. John had even posted the ultrasound she'd had revealing the baby's sex to them. Proud father, something I couldn't make him. She tossed her phone across her bed.

What does it matter, she told herself. It's not like I even love him anymore. And the good thing, she thought as she wiped the lone tear from her cheek, is that my inability to bear children revealed to me the man that John truly is. A cheater. A liar. A disgusting, self-centered, egocentric prick. Definitely not someone she really wanted to be married to. Someone she'd naively placed her trust in who had utterly devastated and backstabbed her. Someone – she jolted from the actual stab of pain in her chest – who just might be capable of deceit and betrayal to this very day. My God, Piper gasped. Maybe, just maybe, Sawyer is right about who he saw in the cottage that afternoon.

But, she mused, lying back on her pillow and tangling her fingers in her disheveled hair, it just didn't make sense. John had given her this ranch as part of their divorce settlement. He'd never wanted it himself, so why scheme to take it away from her now? Becky. Maybe his new woman wanted it for some reason. What better place to raise a child than in the unpolluted countryside on a vast, beautiful ranch? Could this be it, Piper wondered, searching her memories of her life with John. She was trying to reconcile what Sawyer saw, if it really was John he saw. Maybe John's new squeeze was costing him more than he'd bargained for. Piper never had rich tastes, so to speak, but maybe his new soon-to-be-wife did. Maybe this relationship had placed John deep in debt somehow, and he needed or wanted to take back possession of the ranch to sell it and pay off his debts.

The possibilities were endless, the conjectures unlimited, but she knew she'd never get her answer staying up late, fretting in the dark. John certainly wouldn't admit to anything if it had been him in the cottage. And speaking to either Noah or Job was simply out of the question. All I know for sure, Piper finally concluded, is that Sawyer is certain that the man in the cottage with Noah and Job was John, whether mistakenly or not. Sawyer's not lying to me if he really believes it, Piper concluded. At least, unlike my ex-husband, he's being as honest as he can be.

Just as she verged on actually forgiving him, another irritating thought flashed through her mind. Sawyer wouldn't even consider the possibility that he was wrong. Her mother once told her that strong, honorable men are never so inflexible and confident that they won't admit to their mistakes. Is this the type of man she was falling in love with?

She sat bolt upright in bed. *Falling in love with.* She'd said it, at least to herself. She groaned, threw the covers off, and headed downstairs to have something to drink to settle herself down. Tea? Coffee? Hot chocolate, she pondered as she made her way down the stairs. No, she huffed. Her whirling thoughts could only be quieted by a good, stiff drink. Pouring herself a double shot of whiskey in the dining room, she considered going into the kitchen for some ice. Somehow, it seemed like too much trouble in her anxiety, so she pulled up a chair where she was and sat down to sip. One sip quickly turned into another, and before she knew it, she was on her second double shot. If nothing else, it dulls my senses and quiets my thoughts.

It was nearly two hours later when she looked at the wall clock and decided she'd better go back to bed. She had an errand to run in town tomorrow, and she didn't want to sleep in. Back in her bedroom a few minutes later, she miserably realized that the whiskey hadn't done the trick. She was tired, and the world was a little fuzzy, but her anxiety still ran rampant along with her disconcerting thoughts. Why in the hell can't I just leave this alone? Considering going back downstairs to grab the bottle, she decided instead just to get out of bed early and get a head start on her day. It was 4:45 a.m.

She took her time in the shower. The grocery store in town wouldn't open for another three hours and also because the warm water sluicing over her felt so good. If only she could wash her anxieties away so easily, along with the new, menacing feeling of doom. If that *was* John, she considered, he's not about to give up on his schemes. If anything, he'd always seen being thwarted in any way as an extra, more exciting challenge. And if it wasn't him she had to worry about, she still had to worry about Noah and Job. Now, without Sawyer by my side to help me…She cut off the thought before it got her any more depressed.

By the time she heard the men heading towards the house for breakfast, she'd already warmed up what she'd prepared for them the night before. She was dressed and writing out her grocery list at the kitchen table when she heard them approach. Leaping up to get out of the room before Sawyer entered, she accidentally flicked her pen across the room. Dammit! She ran to grab it and fumbled to pick it up off the floor when Sawyer walked in.

"You're up early. That's good. I really need to talk to you."

Forty-Two

SHE'D INSISTED she couldn't stick around because she had an errand to run, but Sawyer pushed the matter, putting her on the spot in front of the men. "Your groceries can wait for a bit," he had told her and offered to speak with her in the dining room while the men ate in the kitchen. With everyone in the room overhearing their conversation, she really didn't have the option of declining without looking stupid or inept, or sending out red flags that something was wrong.

"Fine," she acquiesced and headed hesitantly into the dining room with Sawyer close on her heels.

"Piper," he looked at her evenly as he sat down at the table across from her, "it's about the ranch. The renovations are just about halfway done."

"Oh, wonderful!" she looked both surprised and relieved.

Seriously, Sawyer thought to himself, what the hell did she think I wanted to talk to her about? He'd told himself earlier that he was done with the topic of the cottage's mystery man.

"Here," he laid out diagrams and lists in front of her. "The electrician and plumber are done, and here's what we have left to build in the barn."

He pointed to sketches of the layout of the rest of the stalls, squeeze pens, water troughs, and free-range areas for new mothers and their calves.

"Here's where you'll be containing them with beside the barn when they're outside," he pointed to sketches of the pens, as he explained their location and the rationale.

Piper barely heard a word of it, though. She'd lost concentration when he'd said where *you'll* be containing them and not *we'll*. It had really come to that, she agonized, struggling to keep a placid, interested look on her face. Sawyer really didn't consider himself part of the ranch, or her life, anymore. Barely hearing a word of what he was saying, she made sure to nod whenever he stopped talking and looked up at her.

"And here," he pulled out a multi-page document paperclipped together from the bottom of the pile, "is the itemized list, with costs, for the rest of the supplies."

She paged through it quickly to see the total and sighed. Thank God, she thought, I'll have enough to finish all of this, enough to buy a sufficient number of cattle to start my herd, and also enough left to live on until the ranch is up and running. I'm back on my feet again.

"Any questions?" Sawyer was all business.

No smiling, joking, or words of encouragement or congratulations anymore.

"No, no questions for the moment," she answered quickly.

The air was so thick with tension it was like a suffocating, invisible fog.

"All right, great," Sawyer stood. "I'll leave the paperwork here for you to have a closer look at later. I've got all of this information written down for myself."

He turned away from her with a curt nod and strained smile and left the room. Still rattled, she sat. He was really planning on finishing the building and renovations and leaving her. He'd made it quite clear. *You'll*, not *we'll*, she cringed again. All their plans for the future of the ranch, their plans for it together, were now gone. Devastation swept over her in a dark, smothering cloud, and she struggled not to cry, despite the heavy lump in her throat. Somehow, she couldn't even begin to imagine what the ranch would be like one day without him. She couldn't imagine hiring someone to take his place. Or having the same enthusiasm for the ranch once it was up and running without him to run it by her side.

Eventually, she composed herself, remembering her errand, and grabbed her grocery list from the corner of the table where she'd tossed it. Getting off the property for a while would do her some good. She was beginning to believe that. She slowly headed towards town. The day was bright and sunny and warm. Truly the type of day where you got the feeling that absolutely nothing could go wrong. Just relax for once, she told herself. Enjoy the pleasant drive; take your time at the grocery store; maybe even do some extra shopping in the cute little town you're lucky enough to live near. Stop worrying and being so hard on yourself. She pretty well had her new attitude down pat by the time she walked into the grocery store.

Her list was long, but she didn't rush. She gazed around and admired the friendly, welcoming décor. Hmmm, she smirked. She'd never even noticed the decorations on the walls before. A cute, brightly-painted wood-carved scene of barnyard animals grazing and playing beside a big red barn. She filled her cart with lots of fresh meat for the men, vegetables and fruits, and a few kinds of buns and bread. Picking out cartons of eggs and placing them gingerly in the corner of her cart, she mused about one day having her very own chickens to give her this same supply for free, except for the cost of their care and feed. Chickens, she suddenly remembered, that she'd discussed purchasing some with Sawyer. Nope. I'm not going there now, she abruptly cut off the thought.

By the time she sauntered over to the checkout, after stopping at the deli counter for fresh sandwich meats, her cart was so full she could barely push it. But she didn't mind. It's amazing, she mused, what just a little change of attitude will do to your day. She smiled cheerily at the checkout girl as she began placing her items on the conveyer belt. Normally she'd be annoyed at how loudly the teen chewed her bubble gum, but she decided it wasn't going to bother her in the least. She was going to spend the rest of her day being grateful for everything good that she had.

"That'll be $384.28," the girl said as she blew a huge bubble.

"Alrighty," Piper smiled and slid her debit card into the machine.

It turned out the girl's annoying bubble gum was the least of her problems. After a few moments, the girl shook her head and told her that her card was declined.

"Declined?" Piper startled. "That can't be. Maybe I entered my PIN incorrectly. Let me try it again."

"If the PIN was wrong, that would be a different message," the girl said, but Piper ignored her, pulled out her card, pushed it in again, and punched in her numbers when the screen's message requested her PIN.

"Sorry," the girl grimaced, "it's not going through."

"There has to be some mistake," by this point, Piper's heart was racing. "Just give me a second...."

She grabbed her cell from her purse, signed into her bank account online, and checked her balance. Oh. My. God. She could only pay for these groceries if she returned a few items. What the hell had happened to her money? John's accountant should have transferred her next big lump sum for the ranch into her account by now. Remaining as calm as she could to hide her distress, she blurted out some ridiculous, most likely unbelievable story about a mix-up with a bank transfer. She said she'd just put a few items back for now. The next few minutes were a blur as she hastily decided what to leave behind and everyone in line watched her closely. Feeling her face flush with embarrassment, she bemoaned how she'd never get over this.

"Perfect," the girl said after she'd voided the returned items, and Piper had re-entered her PIN after the new amount was rung up.

"So sorry to hold up the line," she mumbled as she rushed out of the store, pushing her slightly less heavy cart as fast as she could.

But embarrassment was the very least of her problems. She had to get to her bank and straighten this out immediately.

Forty-Three

"IS the manager able to see me briefly in between her appointments?!" Piper tried vainly to control the desperation in her voice.

Her bank's customer service receptionist looked up at her sympathetically from her desk.

"I really don't think so," she sighed, "but I can ask Gloria as soon as she's finished up with her current clients."

"Thank you" was a big understatement, considering the way she felt.

Piper felt like her head was about to explode, sitting rigidly on the black vinyl couch in the reception area. Her mind raced with crazy, disjointed thoughts, ominous and frightening scenarios concerning why her monthly money from John hadn't been transferred to her yet. Sawyer's supposed sighting of him in Noah's cottage weighed heavily on her mind. Glancing once again at Gloria within her glass-walled office in the corner of the room, she rejoiced that the couple she'd been meeting with was now standing, shaking hands with her and about to leave. Please, please see me for a few minutes, she prayed, even as the cheery receptionist went into her office to ask.

Piper held her breath as the woman finally returned, with a noncommittal look on her face.

"Gloria can see you for a short time," she announced.

Barely nodding in appreciation, Piper raced into the manager's office, hoping against hope that there would be time to straighten this out before her next clients arrived.

"Thank you so much for seeing me," she said breathlessly. "I'm in a bind of sorts."

After quickly explaining that her account was set up to receive monthly payments from John via his accountant and that the expected payment hadn't arrived, she asked whether there was any way to check into the reason for the delay.

"Well," Gloria began scrolling on her computer and clicking her mouse, "I can certainly see if your payment is delayed due to bank error or issues, but outside of that, I'm afraid there really isn't much I can do."

Seeing Piper's face fall, as a dark cloud of dread and despair enveloped her, Gloria smiled at her kindly.

"Piper, let me see what I'm able to find out."

Barely breathing in between tense gasps for air, Piper sat quietly, continually crossing and uncrossing her legs. She held her hands stiffly on her lap.

"Yes, I do see that money has been transferred to you monthly from John Baker's account via Rowland and Desbarette Accounting Limited. If it had been on the schedule I see here, your funds would have arrived three days ago. I have no authority to speak with the accounting firm," she looked at Piper evenly, "but I can call the institution the funds are coming from to see if this missing payment is the result of some sort of banking delay."

"I'd really appreciate that," Piper answered quickly, hoping she sounded more stable than she felt.

The minutes ticked by excruciatingly slowly as Gloria Steadman did her best to reach someone at John's bank. Not just anyone, but someone who could help. Sliding the tiny glass bowl of multi-colored mints on the corner of her desk towards Piper, the manager plucked one out to munch on as she sat back in her chair, on hold once again. She has the patience of a saint, Piper thought as she gestured no thank you to the mints. Well, of course, she does, she pondered. It's not *her* sole income that's at stake. A few times, Piper had to control herself from interrupting as Gloria explained the situation to each new person on the other end. They don't need extraneous information. She's got this, Piper attempted to console herself. Just let her do her job.

"Oh...oh, I see...." Gloria nodded, she made brief notations on her yellow notepad. "All right, I understand. Thank you for your help."

As soon as the manager looked towards her, Piper knew that it wasn't good news, based on her gaze.

"I was able to find out that the account your money is being transferred from has insufficient funds. As such, they are unable to send your allotted payment."

"Insufficient funds?! That can't be," Piper leaned forward nervously. "This money is coming from my ex-husband...well, soon to be ex-husband, but it's part of our divorce settlement, and he's very, very wealthy. There is absolutely no way that he's lacking the resources."

"I'm sorry, Piper," Gloria's expression had taken on a pitying air. "I have no way, nor do I have the authority, of checking into your ex-husband's financial situation as a whole. All I can tell you for certain is that neither he, nor his accountant, have deposited sufficient funds into the account they've allotted for your transfers."

The declaration felt like a steel door slamming in her face. Piper sat there uncomfortably, at a loss for words. The manager couldn't help her directly, but she did dole some advice.

"Perhaps you can give your ex-husband a call to determine what the problem is. Or, even better, if you've retained a lawyer, have your lawyer inquire with your ex's attorney on your behalf."

"Yes, yes I will. Thank you so much, Gloria, for your help," Piper stood up slowly, her legs shaking.

Subsequent events were a mere blur to her. Later, she barely remembered shaking Gloria's hand as she shuffled from her office almost blindly to her truck. She sat in the driver's seat for a good ten or fifteen minutes, trying to calm her mind, to keep from sobbing, and to determine what to do. Her lawyer, James Garrett, was a quick ten-minute drive away, but she seriously doubted he could see her on such short notice. She had to speak to him right away.

Grasping at straws, Piper fumbled her phone from her purse. The law secretary scarcely had time to ramble off her usual telephone greeting before Piper jumped in.

"Yes, Audrey, I'm so sorry to interrupt. This is Piper Baker. Is Mr. Garrett available to speak with me?"

"Oh, hello, Piper. No, I'm terribly sorry. James isn't in the office at the moment. I can certainly leave him a message if you like."

"Yes, please. It's extremely urgent. I need to talk to him as soon as possible, hopefully, today."

"I'm expecting him back within the next hour or two, but he does have some appointments, so I can't promise that he'll be able to get back to you today, but I will certainly request that he try."

It was the best she could hope for. After thanking her for her help, Piper hung up her phone and tossed it back into her purse. There was nothing else to do at this point but to head home. Home. Even the word felt like another door slamming, another cruel slap in her face. How long would she be able to hang onto Baker Ranch with no money? It was paid for, free and clear, a very long time ago. However, still, a half-renovated ranch with no cattle or other income couldn't remain in her possession forever. There were other bills for upkeep, Piper winced, for my own survival, and property taxes to pay.

What the hell was she going to do?

Forty-Four

PIPER HAD JUST FINISHED PUTTING away the last of the groceries when her cell phone rang. James Garrett on call display. Yes! Her heart skipped a beat as she answered. As happy as she was to speak with him, she was also filled with dread. Lawyers weren't faith healers or magicians, and there was only so much that he could do for her. She needed to get to the bottom of this latest fiasco with John, but she was also afraid of what she'd find out.

"Hello, Piper. Is everything all right? Audrey told me you were beside yourself when you called. I'm back in my office a little early, so I have a few minutes to chat. What's going on?"

She almost didn't know where to start. She began her explanation by relating her upsetting trip to the grocery store, then followed up with what her bank manager had been able to find out.

"There is absolutely no way in hell that John is out of money, believe me. Trust me, he has the funds, but for whatever reason, neither he nor his accountant has put them into that bank account."

She flinched as she suddenly thought of the cottage and Sawyer's vehement assertion that John was the mystery man. Should she let her lawyer know that there was a possibility that her ex was working very hard against her? As she thought it over, trying to listen to her attorney speak to her at the same time, she realized, for the first time, that she now leaned towards believing Sawyer was accurate regarding whom he saw.

"...it may take some time."

"I'm sorry, what?" Piper apologized.

Mired deep within her perplexing thoughts, she hadn't heard a word of what her lawyer said.

"Where did I lose you?" he asked.

"Oh, Mr. Garrett, I'm sorry. I'm just so upset, and I was thinking about whether to also tell you about something else. I'm afraid you'll have to repeat yourself. I apologize."

"What else do you wish to tell me?"

"Oh, well, just that...it's a bit long and complicated," she began, wondering if she should admit to Sawyer breaking into the cottage to steal her paperback back.

In the end, she decided that he couldn't truly help her if he didn't know everything. She started by recounting how she had been robbed and ended with Sawyer spying on the men in the cottage and stealing all her documents back. Hesitantly, she told him that her ranch hand was one hundred percent certain that the man he saw in the cottage with Noah and Job was her husband, John.

"I see," James paused for what seemed like an eternity as he pondered everything he'd been told. "Whether or not the man in the cottage was John is irrelevant at this point. To be honest, I'm unsure whether it will be relevant at all. There is no law preventing John from creating liaisons or ties with your neighbor, however contentious your relationship with your neighbor may be. However, what concerns me is your missing payment and the apparent reason for it. Piper," he paused, "you really should have retained an attorney while making this agreement with your husband. Although his attorney is obviously aware of it, I'm uncertain whether it is legally binding, as your husband expressed his *intentions* to pay you on paper. Still, there were no signatures obtained to cement the deal. And, let me be very clear. Your husband's attorney is working solely on your husband's behalf, for his benefit alone, not yours."

"So, you're basically saying I'm screwed?" Piper asked, too upset to word it any other way.

"Well, let's hope not," her lawyer chuckled, not in a mean or condescending way, but in a manner to lighten the mood. "As I was saying earlier, in my comments that you missed, I will contact John's attorney to determine what exactly is going on. It may take some time to reach him and for me to hear back."

"Can you do anything to make him pay?" she was desperate.

"That depends on his reasons for not paying. And, of course, whether he and his lawyer decide to honor your rather informal agreement. Leave it with me, Piper. I will attempt to reach John's attorney this afternoon. I'll be in touch with you as soon as I hear anything concrete back."

Even though she'd never mastered the fine art of patience, Piper resolved to try and stay as busy as she could. After all, John's lawyer, Matthew Stephens, couldn't avoid her own attorney forever. Whether that turned out good or bad remained to be seen. Over the next few days, Piper agonized over additional questions she should have asked James Garrett. Not wanting to bother him with them before he had gotten back to her, she decided to jot them down. None were critically important. He was already working on the one question she desperately needed an answer to. Where were her delayed funds?

When he called her a few days later, she held her breath.

"I'm afraid the news isn't good, Piper," he began. "It seems that John has incurred a very large debt, one that you are also responsible for, unfortunately, because legally you are still his wife. As such, Matthew Stephens has informed me in writing that John cannot maintain his previously intended support. There isn't any more money available to you at all."

Piper's world shattered. All her hopes and dreams, her wonderful new life, had been yanked out from under her. Although her attorney tried to calm her as best he could, he didn't succeed. Neither did his advice. Other than that, she should perhaps find another source of income since her husband's money had run dry. After thanking him for his diligence in providing her with an answer, she hung up the phone and went straight to the liquor cabinet in the dining room.

What does it matter if I get drunk? It's not like I have anything much to maintain anymore or anything to really look forward to. She guzzled a straight shot of whiskey and then another before retreating to her room. Amazingly, she did get up in time to make a somewhat drab and incomplete dinner for the men. But only because she wanted to avoid cooking it later, with Sawyer by her side. That evening, her absence from supper went unnoticed because it had become the norm. If Sawyer or any of his crew noticed that dinner was unusually badly prepared, they didn't say anything. It was only after many such lack-luster and skimpy meals that Sawyer saw the red flags. Something other than Piper's existing anger with him concerning John was up.

Forty-Five

ALTHOUGH HE WANTED to give Piper her privacy to work out whatever new concern was bothering her, he had no choice but to go into the house a few days later to talk to her. He would have intercepted her, had she gone out to the barn or even outside to sweep the porch, but she hadn't left the house in days. No errands. No walks. Nothing. Dinner had been over a few hours ago, and he'd cleaned up the kitchen before retreating to his own cottage to catch up on paperwork. As scarce as Piper had made herself, she would have no choice but to talk to him. It was time to pick up more lumber and supplies.

As he walked through the living room, the house was incredibly silent, looking for her. Usually, she had the television or the radio on, even when she was curled up with a good book on the couch.

"Piper?" he called out to her as he slowly ascended the stairs.

Could she have gone to bed already? It was only just past eight o'clock.

"Down here," her voice was hoarse and weary.

She was in the dining room. As soon as he saw her, he knew she'd been drinking. Her eyes were glossed over with what his work crew always referred to as "whiskey fog."

"What do you want?" she slurred as he walked into the room.

Taken aback for a second, he stammered, then regained control of himself.

"It's time to order more supplies."

She laughed. Staring at her in disbelief, he had no idea what she found so funny. Then realized by the mournful and bitter look on her face that she really didn't find it humorous at all.

"How much money do you need this time? Hundreds? Thousands?!" she slurred.

"I'll come back in the morning," he announced, deciding there was no point in talking to her concerning the renovations. She was probably too intoxicated to even spell her own name.

"Oh, yeah?" she snapped. "And just what do you think will be different then?"

"You'll be sober," he said sternly.

She leaped from her chair, and for a second, he thought she was going to attack him. But she merely stumbled to the liquor cabinet to fill her empty glass. It slipped from her fingers and fell to the floor, bouncing across the rug. She bent to retrieve it but fell.

"Piper!" he rushed to her aid, and with great difficulty, helped her to stand.

"Get my glass!" she ordered. "I need another drink."

"No, you don't," he grabbed her shoulders as she tottered, about to fall back down. "You've had quite enough. The only thing you need is to go to bed and sleep this off."

Against her loud and belligerent protests, he guided her up the stairs. He was sure he'd have to argue with her to get her to lie down, but, surprisingly, she saw her bed and dove upon it. She was nearly asleep by the time he finished straightening her blankets, pulling them gently on top of her. Whatever the hell is going on, he thought, I guess I'll find out tomorrow *if,* by some miracle, she actually decides to confide in me.

Forty-Six

IRONICALLY, as Piper slept like a baby, Sawyer lay awake for most of the night. Has she relapsed into drinking, he wondered because she's still so upset about my insistence that it's John I saw in the cottage? Maybe, he sat up as he thought of it. Maybe she's actually found a way to confirm that it was! Whatever had caused her recent plunge back into alcoholism was also affecting her daily routines and tasks. The more he considered and thought about it, the more worried he became. He was used to her not speaking to him and to her absence at meals, but he found it more than disconcerting that she hadn't left the house at all. And, a few of the men had asked him why their recent suppers were so lacking in preparation and volume these days.

Vowing to get clear answers tomorrow, he dolefully pulled the covers up over his head. Although that blocked the moonlight streaming through the window, it did nothing to stop his disquieting dreams. When he finally went into the farmhouse the next afternoon, not too early because he knew Piper needed to sleep off the whiskey, he felt as tired and distraught as Piper looked.

She was sitting at the kitchen table, drinking hot chocolate despite the blistering warmth of the day. Not a good sign, he mused, and without saying anything, he pulled up a seat. She was going to talk to him about whatever it was that was bothering her, whether she liked it or not.

"You were here last night, weren't you?" she asked, her voice still clouded from last night's binge.

"Yup, I was," he smirked at her.

There was no sense in giving her hell because she was apparently struggling within a hell all her own.

"Was I rude to you?"

"You mean ruder than normal?" he chuckled.

"I guess I deserved that," she shook her head.

"What's going on, Piper? Despite you trying so damn hard to push me away, we're not exactly strangers. You can talk to me."

"Oh, Sawyer, I don't even know where to start!" she burst into tears. "It's John. It's *everything*! My whole world has fallen apart."

She told him about the missing payment and how there wouldn't be any more money at all. Not for the supplies they needed. Not for monthly bills. Not even for any more food. Ah, now this makes sense, he mused, thinking of their recent skimpy meals.

"What's worse is that I have absolutely no solution, and neither has my lawyer at this point. I'm equally responsible for John's debt because we're still legally married. And because I didn't have my own lawyer when John and I made the agreement about his lump sum monthly payments, and there were no signatures obtained, James Garrett feels that, even if we uncovered some more of John's money, which is unlikely, we'd have no way of making him pay."

The new reality hit Sawyer hard. It was Piper's reality and problem, but it was also his. He realized at that moment just how deeply entwined he considered his life with hers. The ranch wasn't just her dream. It had become his as well. Not because he needed his ongoing job as ranch manager – with his skills, he could find work anywhere – but because Piper's wellbeing and happiness mattered to him more than anything else. And because he wanted her to have a wonderful, stable, and happy life with him at her side. Without giving it another second's thought, he leaned across the table and grasped her hand.

"You don't need John's money, Piper. *We* don't need John's money to make this work. Listen, I've got some money saved up. After Peggy-

Lee died, I worked as hard as possible to avoid doing or thinking about anything else. I virtually had no responsibilities left, so I could pocket and keep most of what I made. And I have the majority of my salary that you've paid me. After all, I've been living here and eating for free. I'll give you what I have. It'll be enough to finish the renos and buy cattle to get the ranch going until it maintains itself. You can just start paying me back slowly once the money from the ranch starts rolling in."

"My God, Sawyer, I can't let you do that! It's way, way too generous, and I just won't risk taking all your money and putting you in a bind. Besides," her expression darkened, and her eyes welled with tears, "I've already decided that this time, I really am going to sell the ranch."

"You're *not* selling the ranch," Sawyer squeezed her hand. "Not after everything you've already gone through to hold on to it and to begin building it up to what it was. Don't worry about my money. What else, really, do I have to spend it on?"

"Um, maybe yourself," she smiled.

"My life is here, though, on this ranch with you. So..." he smiled back at her as he leaned across the table, "by giving you the money, I really am spending it on myself."

Well, if that wasn't a twist of words and a great argument, nothing was. She laughed.

"So, I guess we're talking again?" she looked downright mischievous.

"You bet."

They were still sitting at the table, discussing all the details, when they heard a vehicle coming up her driveway.

"You expecting anyone?" she asked him.

"No. Besides, they're not heading to the barn. Sounds like they're coming to the house."

"It better not be Noah!" Piper moaned as she stood up.

They walked outside to stand on the porch just as the car slowed to a stop. Sawyer didn't recognize it, but Piper did. John slithered out of his Audi with a cynical smile on his face. Sawyer heard Piper gasp quietly beside him. Stepping protectively in front of her, he blocked John's way up the porch steps.

"What do you want here?" he sneered.

Forty-Seven

"WHAT I WANT HERE IS to talk to Piper!" John scowled.

Piper gasped as he rushed towards Sawyer, thinking he would barrel into him or try to shove him aside. Instead, he brushed roughly by him and stomped up the porch steps to stop only inches away from her. Still frozen in place from the shock of his arrival, she held her ground.

"Let's go inside, Piper," John said as genially as he could. "I came to speak with you, not your ranch hand. What I have to say has nothing to do with him and is none of his concern."

From the corner of her eye, Piper discerned Sawyer moving towards them. She was petrified things would erupt into a physical fight. Although she wanted to avoid that at all costs, she also didn't want to be alone and vulnerable with John.

"If it's about the ranch, I'd prefer to talk out here. And it does concern, Sawyer. As my ranch manager, he also needs to know what's going on."

"Ranch *manager*?" John's expression darkened for a moment, slipped into anger, and then quickly into a condescending smirk. "Whatever you wish to call him, then. Fine."

The three of them stood silently for a moment, eyeing each other uncomfortably until John finally spoke again.

"You're well aware that I know of the financial bind you're in at present. I came here to discuss that with you and kindly offer a solution. It's the very least that I can do."

Piper's nerves, already coiled tightly, threatened to spring. It was all she could do to control herself and keep her emotions in check. At least as much as she was able to.

"My financial bind, as you call it, is all your fault! Do you really expect me to believe, even for an instant, that you're here to help?!"

He chuckled. That same arrogant, aloof snicker that she remembered and hated so well.

"Piper, as argumentative and defiant as always," his smile didn't match his tone. "The fact that it is all my fault, as you say, is the very reason I am here. Unfortunately, the enormous debt makes it impossible for me to support you and your renovation and the maintenance of this ranch." His cold eyes sparkled as he continued, "However, I can offer you my assistance by taking the ranch off your hands."

"Oh, really?" Piper sneered. "And just how in the hell do you plan to do that? And why?"

"Think of it as a final act of kindness," he lifted his arm, about to pat her on the shoulder, but quickly lowered it, thinking twice. "I've unavoidably placed you in a terrible bind, which," he paused for effect, "can be alleviated when I generously purchase the ranch from you."

Piper felt like she'd been punched in the gut. She heard Sawyer grunt quietly beside her, but he said nothing. John stared at her, unblinking, waiting for her response. He was stunned when it came.

"You're absolutely the very last person I would ever sell this ranch to, closely seconded by Noah Martinez. Thanks for your trumped-up concern, but I've already gotten things figured out."

"Oh?" John grimaced, unable to hide his disappointment and surprise.

If he's waiting for an explanation, he's not going to get it, Piper thought as she glared at him. Sawyer was thinking the same thing, standing tall to her left and quickly moving beside her. Their solution was none of John's business at all.

"Don't think for a second that I don't know what you're doing. There was absolutely no large debt while we were together or even when we discussed and made the divorce settlement. And I'm also well aware of your little deal with Noah and that you're behind my stolen documents."

He hesitated for a second, thinking he might deny everything she'd said. Then thought better of it. Piper had always been stubborn and strong-willed. And, in John's eyes, she had an incredibly annoying and inflexible mind of her own. He could argue; he could deny, but it would do no good. He decided to take a different approach.

"I see that, as always, you've woven quite a tale within your own mind. Luckily, our relationship is over, and I no longer have to disagree or argue with you. You're totally free to think whatever you want. John stepped closer to Piper, causing Sawyer to place his hand protectively on her shoulder. "My offer is time-sensitive, just in case your own solution to your dilemma doesn't work out."

"And just why wouldn't it?" she hissed, wishing she could spit in his face instead.

"Things happen," he answered softly. "Unforeseen things. Life has an uncanny way of throwing curveballs."

"That's enough!" Sawyer pulled Piper towards him as he snarled at John. "If that's a threat...."

"Threat? Don't be ridiculous," his eyes narrowed. "I have absolutely no reason to make threats. I'm here making a legitimate offer as an act of kindness, since I'm unintentionally responsible for Piper's financial dilemma."

"Right," Piper jeered. "And we're supposed to believe you're somehow suddenly in dire financial straits and that you had nothing to do with Noah and his henchmen stealing all my documents."

"We?" John snickered. "Now it's not just you, Piper? It's you and Sawyer, I see."

If looks could kill, both she and Sawyer would have crumpled to the ground dead."

"Yes, *we!*" Piper barely hesitated before taking back control of the conversation. "Sawyer is my ranch manager and, if you haven't noticed, you're here talking to both of us."

"Of course," John huffed, then hesitated for a second. "Then let me make it very clear *to both of you*. You have absolutely no proof of anything you so carelessly accuse me of. Nothing. Not one iota of fact to back up your accusations. In any case, you've made your position clear. We're done here. My offer to help you is withdrawn."

He turned abruptly and headed for the porch steps.

"And like I could have trusted your offer anyway!" Piper yelled after him. "Your offer is about as trustworthy as you are. Which means it's worth nothing. Nothing at all."

John turned towards her, no longer sporting the cynical smile.

"You best be on your way. Now!" Sawyer yelled.

Glancing disdainfully at him for a second, John turned back to Piper.

"Well," he started, "now that I know you think so little of me, let me make myself even more clear." John leaned forward, the veins visibly pulsing in his neck, "I'll make sure you're left with absolutely *nothing* to remember me by," he seethed. "Not one red cent of my money and certainly not one blade of grass on this ranch."

Literally stunned by his open malevolence, Piper merely stared at him in shock. Sawyer moved up behind her, wrapping his arm protectively around her waist. Without a word to each other, they watched John stomp to his Audi and take off, screeching the tires long after he'd pulled out onto the highway.

Forty-Eight

IT TOOK Piper all afternoon to even begin to calm down. Sawyer had done all he could to reassure her that John couldn't do anything to them and that everything would be all right. Still, she couldn't shake the ominous feeling that things were about to get much, much worse. She'd been married to John long enough to know how determined and creative he was when he really wanted something. He'd never once gone after anything he didn't get in the end. This, of course, made him an exceptionally successful businessman. But it also deemed him a formidable and dangerous foe.

"I guess you're not hungry tonight?" Sawyer tried to sound light-hearted as he walked through the kitchen door.

"Oh, my goodness! I haven't even started supper," Piper leaped up from her seat. "The pork chops are thawed. I just have to throw them on the barbecue. And I guess some potatoes too, and I'll have to warm up some canned beans."

"I'll help you," Sawyer smiled cheerfully. "We'll get dinner ready in plenty of time before the men finish working in the barn."

Rescued again, Piper thought gratefully as she wrapped the potatoes in tin foil. Sawyer was throwing the chops onto the barbecue. What would I do without him, she wondered, sure that by now, her life would have totally fallen apart. He'd jumped in front of her when Noah shot at them. He'd retrieved her stolen documents, and now he was paying for everything, keeping the ranch afloat until it made money to support itself. Unless John somehow managed to throw a wrench into their plans.

Try as she might, she just couldn't stop thinking of her ex-husband and his threats. Although Sawyer seemed one hundred percent confident that there was nothing John could do to them, she remained more than a little uncertain. I know him, really know him, and Sawyer doesn't know what John is truly capable of, she thought. Wincing, she remembered her own naïveté not so long ago; when she'd first discovered John's infidelity and when his mask of integrity, loyalty, and honor – and love – began to slip away. Still shocked at how much John hated her now, she dreaded his next move.

"You want me to put the beans on the stove?" Sawyer's voice startled her.

She'd been standing at the kitchen counter deep in thought and clutching the plates of potatoes in her hands. Sawyer took them from her to put them on the barbecue, as she said she'd handle the beans. Looking at her curiously for a moment, he decided not to say anything. At least not until after dinner, when they had more time to talk.

A little later, watching the men eagerly pile food onto their plates, Piper realized how hungry she'd kept them since her horrible day at the bank. Today, Sawyer had insisted they prepare a generous, hearty meal because he was covering the cost from here on in. Looking around at the men joking and laughing, she felt incredibly guilty for not feeding them properly. As well as incredibly grateful that they were totally oblivious to what had gone on.

She didn't have much of an appetite but moved her food around her plate dutifully every time Sawyer looked at her. With any luck, he wouldn't notice how little she'd eaten when dinner concluded, and she hid her plate below others as she snatched up the dishes to take to the sink.

"Why don't you just go into the living room and relax," he told her about an hour later, once the men had filed out to go to their rooms.

"I'll get this. You look exhausted. Grab a beer, and I'll join you as soon as I'm done."

"No, I'm not dumping dishwashing duties on you again," she insisted, but he merely laughed.

He grabbed her gently by the shoulders and spun her to face the living room.

"Go!" he pointed and slapped her on the shoulder. "I'll be there in a few minutes."

"Fine," she relented but insisted that she grab that beer he suggested first.

Curling up on the sofa, alone with her thoughts, she realized she didn't feel any better. Not in the least. In the peace and quiet, able to think more clearly, she actually felt much worse. John's visit had really shaken her, and the worst thing about it was that she didn't know what to do. How do you fight against something before it even happens, she pondered, when you don't even know beforehand what it is? By the time Sawyer joined her, she was beside herself once again.

"I see your *me time* to relax hasn't helped you any," he said as he took a seat beside her.

His smile was gone. All Piper could see on his face was worry and concern.

"I'm sorry," she sighed. "But you just don't understand how determined John is when he puts his mind to something. We may think there's nothing he can do, but he'll find a way to get revenge on me and ruin our lives."

"Piper..." Sawyer put his beer down on the table beside hers and moved closer. Pulling her to his chest, he held her tight. "You're talking as if John's some sort of undefeatable monster, but...."

"He is!" she blurted as she moved away from him.

"No," he shook his head slowly. "You only think that because you once trusted him, and you're shocked at the depths of his dishonesty and hatred. And because you've been so hurt."

"Sawyer, what are we going to do?" she fell back into his arms again and laid her head gently on his chest.

"We don't have to do anything," he said calmly, "except stand strong and outwit him again if he, and I doubt it, makes his next move."

Two days later, the game was on again. Piper had just finished vacuuming when her lawyer called. Running to answer her cell that was charging on the kitchen counter, she cringed when she saw James Garrett's name on call display. As soon as he began speaking, his serious, somber tone told her his information would be anything but good.

"I received paperwork today filed by Matthew Stephens, your husband's lawyer, with the courts. John is accusing you of adultery, which his lawyer claims will impact the settlement they previously offered as part of the divorce. Your husband is petitioning to revoke the gifting of his ranch to you. He is asking the courts that you vacate the property within thirty days."

"Oh my God!" Piper screamed.

So much for Sawyer's naïve optimism.

"Piper, please try to remain calm. We will be prepared for this. Have a seat and take some deep breaths, all right? I'm going to ask you some questions so we can begin to build your defense."

"My defense? I haven't done anything! John is just trying to find a new way to take my ranch."

"Then we'll prove that," Garrett responded.

Their next few minutes of conversation were a blur to Piper when she hung up the phone. Luckily, he'd made an appointment to see her in person at the end of the week. With any luck, she'd get better control of herself and gather her thoughts by then.

Forty-Nine

INSTEAD OF FACILITATING Piper to clear her head, the next few days only prolonged her anxiety and agony. With too much time to think, her worst and bleakest thoughts outnumbered even the positive affirmations she tried. The end of the week, and her appointment with her lawyer, couldn't come soon enough.

In her umpteenth effort since James Garrett's call, Piper looked over the notes she'd made of things to discuss with him and the information she'd written down that she thought would help him win her case. Seeing everything listed on paper, in her neat writing, and in point form made it all seem so finite. As if these considerations would make or break her. Period. As if her entire life and future boiled down to this one upcoming court case. Because, of course, it did.

"Still working on that?" Sawyer asked as he walked into the kitchen.

"I haven't stopped, although, since this morning, I haven't written another word."

"Piper," he sighed, pulling up a chair next to her. "Please try to relax. We'll go over this together tonight. And don't forget, your lawyer will have lots of input as well. He's an expert at all of this. You aren't, especially because you're personally involved."

"I know..." she huffed, throwing down her pen. "It's just that everything we've worked for all rests on this case. Our lives, the future, all of our hopes and dreams."

He smiled at her, taking her hand.

"We'll go over this list after supper, I promise. We'll be more than ready for our appointment. Your husband may be smart and determined, but he's also a liar and a crook."

Squeezing her hand as he stood up, he tried, as usual, to lighten the mood.

"But right now, if I don't feed our hungry crew, they're likely to revolt."

Good Lord, she'd done it again. Mired deep in her thoughts and depression, she'd forgotten to prepare another meal.

"Sandwiches all right?" she asked hopefully.

She really didn't have the energy to make a better lunch.

"Yup, I'll help."

Sawyer steered their conversation away from John, lawyers, and court as they prepared the quick meal together. Piper needs a break to clear her thinking, he rationalized, so he talked about how far they'd gotten with the renos and construction in the barn. Although he could tell that Piper was distracted, he persisted. Before meeting with her lawyer, and especially before trial, the last thing she needed was to fizzle and burn out.

However, that evening, he kept his promise to go over her list with her. He was determined to help her make it as complete as possible, give her attorney some ammunition, and so Piper could finally rest.

"We should write down everything we remember about exactly what John said to us."

"Right!" Piper gasped, "Why hadn't I thought of that? Oh, Sawyer, I'm going to be an absolute mess when I take the witness stand."

"No, you won't," he said. "What you'll be is very well-prepared."

"Yeah," she huffed. "A very well-prepared nervous wreck."

As distressing as it was, they went over John's unwelcome visit, from the time he stepped from his car to when he sped off.

"You know, we're also going to be asked some very personal questions," Sawyer said, taking her hand. "By your lawyer tomorrow and by both lawyers in court."

She looked at him questioningly for a moment, then quickly clued in.

"About our relationship. About adultery," she sighed.

"Yes," he nodded. "Not only will they ask us if anything's *happened* between us, but they'll also ask us about the exact nature of our relationship. They'll want to know about my role here on the ranch and about my status in your life."

So, we're having this conversation now, she pondered, before we're even ready. Damn John and his obsessive hatred and greed!

"Piper?" Sawyer interrupted her thoughts. "What are we going to say? I mean, what do you want us to say. I'll go along with you."

Great, she thought. Throw it all in my lap.

"What do you want to say?" she turned the tables.

"The complete truth," he smiled. "You know how I feel about you. At least I hope you do. My future, our future, is here at the ranch together because I love you."

Her smile lit the heavens as she dove into his arms.

"I love you too!"

As they held each other closely for a few minutes, Piper wished their embrace would never end. Finally, Sawyer leaned away and took her hands in his.

"We'll get through this together, I promise," he said.

For the time, she actually began to believe him, that she might keep her ranch and that their plans would work out. By the time they walked into James Garrett's office together, she was filled with optimism. Cautious optimism, but optimism nonetheless.

"There are several factors to consider here," James Garrett tented his fingers together as he leaned forward behind his desk. "First and foremost, the accusation of adultery. You will have to be totally honest with me here, and you must avoid inconsistencies on the witness stand. What exactly is the nature of your relationship?"

"I didn't even meet Sawyer until after John and I separated," Piper began.

She explained how she'd met Sawyer when looking for a ranch hand after John had given her the property. They outlined their progressive relationship, with Piper blushing while explaining that nothing sexual in nature had occurred between them.

"But, you two are in love, correct?" Garrett asked.

"You bet," Sawyer smiled widely as Piper nodded.

"Congratulations," Garrett smiled for the first time since their meeting began. "Make sure you freely and willingly admit that or trust me, John's lawyer will trip you up. There's no adultery here. That's apparent. You and John were long separated, Piper, by the time your relationship with Sawyer began."

"It's John who's committed adultery!" Piper leaned forward in her chair. "I can't even believe he has the balls to accuse me of that...oh, sorry," she smirked, embarrassed. "I won't say *balls* in court."

"Cojones works," Garrett laughed. "Make sure you pronounce it clearly, *ka-hu-nas*, so everyone understands."

This lightened the mood considerably, and Piper giggled as she fished out her cell from her purse. Opening Facebook, she quickly found John's profile and his posts.

"His fiancé is very, very pregnant, and it's evident their baby was conceived while we were still together, while I was still living with John."

"Hmmm, this will be very useful," Garrett smiled, reaching for her phone.

He summoned Audrey, his secretary, and instructed her to scroll through all of John's posts, beginning with when he first mentioned or uploaded photos of his girlfriend.

"Take screenshots right away, in case they're deleted," he told her. "Before Matthew Stephens gets a chance to instruct his client to remove them."

"I'll get this back to you, hopefully before you leave today," she told Piper as she left the room.

"Next," Garrett proclaimed, "We must deal with John's motivation for these adultery claims. Any idea what's behind this, other than just pure malice and hate?"

"Yes, here, Mr. Garrett," Piper said, handing him the notes she'd made. "We've written down everything we remember that John said to us when he showed up at the ranch."

Her notes detailed John's unexpected visit, and right below that,

Garrett read over the information she'd provided concerning the theft of her documents and who Sawyer saw and heard in Noah's cottage. Both she and Sawyer sat quietly, on edge, while her lawyer made some quick notes for himself on the yellow legal pad by his hand.

"And you're absolutely certain it's John you saw there and what you heard them say?" his questions were directed at Sawyer. "John's lawyer will try hard to unnerve you and confuse you on the stand."

"I know that," Sawyer acknowledged as Piper also nodded in understanding. "I'm ready. *We're* ready," he said, glancing at Piper.

But Piper wasn't so sure.

Fifty

SITTING STIFFLY on the vinyl-cushioned bench outside the courtroom, Piper looked down the long hallway again, expecting to see James Garrett arriving. Instead, she was shocked at what she saw. John, holding hands with his new fiancé, Becky. How dare he bring her here?! It was worse than another slap in the face. It amounted to a kick in the gut. She looked away quickly before either of them had seen her peering their way. No way was she going to give them the satisfaction of knowing she was uncomfortably watching their arrival. She stared to her left, at the closed doors of the other courtrooms, trying her best to erase all emotion from her face.

Becky's heels clicked loudly on the tile as she and John got closer. Piper's stomach churned. She had no idea what she'd do or say if they stopped to talk to her. As childish as it was, she wanted nothing more than to knee John in the groin and scratch that bitch's face.

"Mr. Garrett not here yet?"

It was Sawyer. He'd just returned from the bathroom. Piper barely glanced at him as he sat down beside her.

"Don't look to your right," she whispered. "John's headed this way with his girlfriend."

Sawyer's eyes widened, but he didn't turn his head.

"Unbelievable that he'd bring her here!" Piper hissed quietly.

"Maybe she's being called as a witness," Sawyer conjectured just as the couple walked past them straight into the courtroom.

"Ugh. I hadn't thought of that," Piper squirmed.

"It'll be all right. Your lawyer will have it all under control."

He took her hand just as James Garrett emerged from behind a door to the left of their courtroom. Piper surmised that he must have gotten here early and been reading over documents in an adjoining room.

"It's time for us to go in," he nodded towards them. "Just have a seat somewhere near the front, Sawyer, until you're called to testify. Piper, of course, you'll be sitting beside me on our side of the room."

Piper's throat went dry as soon as they entered, and she followed her lawyer to her seat on shaking legs. Stop it, she chided herself angrily. Don't let John do this to you. However, despite her best efforts, her throat remained dry and scratchy, and her vision blurred as she glanced around the room. Becky was seated right behind John's table, looking confident and composed. And young. Damn him, she thought. If he thinks he's going to get away with this, he's wrong. She affirmed silently that the ranch is mine through both lawyers' opening arguments. No way will I let that heartless, evil bastard take it away from me.

Matthew Stephens wasted no time in putting John on the stand. Piper could barely control her rage as questioning progressed.

"So, other than Piper's cold and distant behavior, what made you believe she was having an affair, or series of affairs, throughout the latter part of your marriage?"

"The texts that I saw on her phone. All from men I didn't know and whom she had never mentioned to me. There were very, very friendly exchanges," John looked sincere, "and if I remember correctly, at least a few of them said, 'I love you' back and forth."

"He's lying," Piper tapped her lawyer's arm as she whispered to him. "It's all total bullshit."

He nodded and made some notes.

"Moving forward," Stephens said as he paced in front of the witness stand. "What makes you so sure that Piper is involved in a romantic, possibly sexual, relationship with her ranch hand?"

"I clearly saw them kissing on the porch as I drove up the road towards the farmhouse."

Piper groaned her anger a little too loudly, and Garrett nudged her. She could barely refrain from speaking as John's questioning continued. Looking back on it, she thought she might have lost control if her lawyer hadn't slid a notepad and pen in front of her, instructing her to make notes. It kept her busy and quiet. Garrett was very good at his job.

"In conclusion, why did you gift your ranch to Piper when you believed she'd been unfaithful during your marriage? And why do you wish to take back ownership of the ranch now?"

John leaned forward, placing his hands comfortably on the desk in front of him. He managed to look both wounded and kind.

"To be honest, I felt deeply sorry for Piper. She'd been incredibly depressed and unstable since we'd given up on trying to conceive a child. I believed that the ongoing affairs were a product of her deep-seated insecurities. I did my best to forgive her and provided Piper with a beautiful home once our marriage dissolved."

"And now?" Stephens prodded him.

"And now," John sighed, "I deeply regret my compassion and generosity. I've heard nothing but disturbing things from people I know in and around Cassidy Falls. Even before she took up with her ranch hand, Piper's behavior has been licentious and immoral. I simply no longer wish to give Piper more than she deserves in this divorce."

James Garrett's cross-examination was brutal and thorough. "You're lying, aren't you?" It must have been repeated at least fifty or so times. When questioned about who he knew in Cassidy Falls that had given him unfavorable information about Piper, John, of course, named Noah Martinez, and Job Hernandez, Noah's ranch hand. Piper had no doubt that Martinez and Hernandez had their testimonies well-rehearsed, neither did her lawyer. Unsurprisingly, when asked whether he'd had anything to do with the theft of Piper's documents, John steadfastly denied it. He admitted to visiting with Noah and Job in the cottage, just as Sawyer saw when "trespassing," but he said no paperwork of any sort had been on the premises or involved. Piper prayed the judge would see through him for what he was.

Sawyer's testimony was somewhat briefer, if no less stressful. He admitted to being in a platonic but romantic relationship with Piper now. Still, he vehemently denied that he and Piper had been kissing on the porch just as John arrived. He insisted they never developed anything past friendship if Piper were not already separated and amid a divorce. When questioned about the conversation he overheard in the cottage and elsewhere on Martinez's property, he was adamant. He insisted that he'd clearly heard and understood every word about the robbery and their foiled plans to take Piper's ranch. John's lawyer didn't rattle him regardless of how hard he tried.

Following Noah and Job's testimony, Piper hesitantly took the stand. Stephens' questioning was brutal and demeaning, but she held her own.

"John's lying. It's that simple. There were no texts. No affairs at all on my part while we were married. I have never acted licentiously or immorally in my life, not once. This whole court case is John's last desperate attempt to take away the ranch he's given me. He is the only one in our marriage who cannot be trusted. The only one who's been unfaithful and dishonest to this very day."

When it was Garrett's turn to question her, she relaxed a bit. He clicked the remote in his hand and brought a huge screenshot of John's Facebook account upon the courtroom's big screen.

"Do you recognize this, Piper?" Garrett asked gently.

"Yes, I do. It's a post on John's Facebook, and that is his fiance's ultrasound."

"You're correct. Can you read, for all of us, the date it was posted and what John said?"

She did so dutifully as the courtroom hushed.

"By my calculations, it seems that John and Becky's baby was conceived while he was still married to you. Would you agree with me then, Piper, that John is the one who was unfaithful during your marriage?"

"Yes," she sighed.

His questioning concluded shortly after, and, following his closing arguments, he rested his case. Matthew Stephens was relentless during his final remarks, leaving both Piper and Sawyer praying that the judge would see through everything and favor their side of the case. As it was,

Judge Eldridge called an hour and a half long recess to decide. Piper and Sawyer waited tensely with James Garrett in the adjacent meeting room.

"I'm nervous and petrified," Piper told Garrett as she drummed her fingers on the table. "Not that you didn't do a fantastic job, it's just that John is such a great liar, and Noah and Job are backing him up."

"I know, Piper," he nodded gently. "As I said, you never know which way things will go in court, but if the worst happens, remember, we can always appeal."

Groaning, she shook her head mournfully. She honestly had no idea whether she could go through another horrible trial. Just as she was about to tell him that, Sawyer entered the room. He'd slipped away quickly to bring them all lunch. After unwrapping the paper from around her submarine, she stared at it blankly. There was no way she could eat. When the bailiff came in over an hour later to call them back into the courtroom, her sub was still sitting in front of her, untouched. Each minute that ticked by after they took their seats seemed like an hour. She was about to jump out of her skin.

"All rise."

Judge Eldridge entered solemnly. There was no way to read his face. Piper swallowed hard and held her breath.

Fifty-One

"IN CONCLUSION, we are left with contradictory testimony; we only have proof of John Baker's infidelity. No such proof has been established on the part of his wife. As such," he glared at Matthew Stephens, "this case is dismissed."

Piper gasped loudly, barely stopping herself from leaping out of her seat to give both her attorney and Sawyer a hug. She was overcome by tears of happiness for most of their drive home together. Thankfully, she was a passenger, and Sawyer had the wheel.

"I told you, Piper, that everything would be all right!" Sawyer smiled as they turned into the driveway of the ranch.

"Yup, you did," she laughed happily, "but you didn't actually know it till Judge Eldridge made his decision. Admit it, now that the case is over. You weren't as sure of the outcome as you made out."

"Nope," his smile widened as they got out of her truck. "I'll never admit to not having unending faith in a happy future for us."

"Fine, whatever," she smirked. Looking around outside just before they went in the front door, she exclaimed, "Isn't this ranch the most beautiful and perfect property in the entire world?!"

"Sure is," Sawyer gave her a big hug before swinging open the door.

"After you," he said, gesturing her forward, making a big deal of their entrance into their home.

They spent the evening watching television and eating popcorn after wolfing down huge helpings of leftovers. The men had made their own supper, and each left a large plateful of roast beef, mashed potatoes, and corn. It seemed Piper was suddenly ravenous after missing lunch. As well as very tired. She fell asleep with her head on Sawyer's shoulder long before the movie ended. He woke her gently, not wanting her to awake later with a sore neck.

"It's late anyway, Piper. Why don't we just get some sleep."

She agreed quickly and shuffled off to bed as Sawyer walked out the door to go to his cottage, flicking off the last of the lights. Once upstairs, Piper had a burst of energy after lying down on her bed. The lamp on her nightstand illuminated her painting of the horses across the room, and she smiled. This really was her home now, despite her parents' trepidations before she left. Glancing at the clock on the nightstand, she decided it wasn't too late in the evening to give her mom a long-overdue call.

"Piper, what's wrong?" her mom's familiar voice rang out from her cell.

"Mom! Nothing's wrong. What a way to answer your phone."

"I knew it was you. I have call display, Piper, and you never call me this late."

"It's only ten o'clock, mom."

"I rest my case."

Piper laughed. It actually felt good to know that her mom was worried about her and that she cared so much. It's time for a little bit, or a lot, of honesty, she decided.

"Well, actually, mom, there's been a lot going on...."

She filled her in about everything that had happened after she arrived at the ranch, including the mysterious fire in the barn. By the time she detailed today's court case, her mother was beside herself.

"And you didn't think of telling your father any of this or me?! Why, for heaven's sake?"

"I didn't want to worry you, and," she paused, trying to find the right words, "I wanted to be truly independent for once and do things on my own."

"Piper, you've been an independent and very headstrong, I may add, child all your life!"

"But I'm not a child anymore, mom. That's the key. The bottom line is that you and dad have always taken care of me, and while I was married, John did too. I've never truly taken care of myself or fully made my own choices and decisions. This was my chance, and I didn't want to screw it up."

After a brief pause, her mother asked if she was happy now that the worst seemed to be over and she had control of her life.

"Happier than I've ever been," she replied. "And I've met someone."

"You have? Already?" her mom was surprised.

"Not on purpose. Not as a crutch or a rebound, if that's what you're thinking. I met Sawyer when I hired him to work for me. He's my ranch manager now."

Her mom listened intently as Piper told her all about him.

"He sounds like everything John is *not*," her mom exclaimed. They both laughed and agreed how fantastic that was.

"I can hardly wait to meet him," her mom nudged, and shortly afterward they ended their call.

"You will soon," Piper promised her. "Just as soon as we get the renovations finished, we'll come for a visit, or you and dad can come here."

"I'm holding you to that," her mom laughed as they said goodbye.

Finally, things are starting to get better. Piper smiled as she turned off the light, laid down, and closed her eyes.

Fifty-Two

SHE AWOKE to the savory smells of bacon and coffee wafting upstairs from the kitchen. Being relieved of the huge weight and stress from her shoulders, she'd finally been relaxed enough to make up for all the lost sleep. Feeling guilty, she threw her robe and slippers on and made her way downstairs. Sawyer would have had to make everyone's breakfast all by himself, again.

"Oh, Ms. Baker, you're here. Congratulations!" Tim said as he stood quickly and pulled out a chair for her at the table.

Sawyer was just grabbing more orange juice from the fridge. She looked at him questioningly, disturbed and irritated for a moment, thinking he'd told the men about her husband's adultery accusation and her winning the court case.

"I've told the guys we are now officially more than three-quarters of the way through rebuilding and renovations. It's time to celebrate how far we've come," he smiled.

"Oh, of course!" she exhaled.

There was nothing like looking like a deer in headlights, she smirked as she took her seat.

"So, boss man," Will laughed, "are we going to have a good old-fashioned country hoedown with square dances and everything?"

"Nah," Sawyer smiled. "I thought I'd just give you guys a few days off after today and an extra week's pay as a bonus on your next check."

"That'll do, that'll do!" Mike whistled. "Ain't none of us going to complain about that!"

"The hoedown," Sawyer said as he spooned sugar into his coffee, "will be our first plan of action once we completely finish everything."

Piper was so happy; she ate much more than usual. Her appetite had finally come back. After breakfast, as the men filed out of the kitchen, she pulled Sawyer close to her, not caring anymore if someone saw.

"Why didn't you tell me the remodel was so far along?"

"Wanted to surprise you and cheer you up."

To his dismay, Piper's expression darkened.

"You didn't want to say anything in case I lost in court and lost the ranch, after we'd come this far."

She knew him better than he'd thought.

"Well, we don't have to worry about anything like that anymore," he said as he wrapped his arms tightly around her.

She didn't hug back.

"Well, let's just not screw it up in the final innings," she sighed. "Sawyer, are you sure we can afford to give all the men an extra week's pay?"

"I'm sure. One hundred percent," he nodded. "I told you we have more than enough money, and I meant it. Don't worry. I know what I'm doing. I've been a boss before. This type of motivation, at this stage, lights a fire under work crews' butts. They'll work even faster and harder now, and we'll be done everything in no time flat."

"OK," she smiled. "I'll leave the crew up to you."

Because she'd slept in and forced him to make breakfast on his own, she refused to let him help her with the dishes.

"You just get back to what's more important," she laughed, slapping him playfully on the butt.

"My, my, Ms. Baker. You're getting awfully frisky," he laughed. "Careful now, I can easily get used to that!"

"Out!" she joked, pointing towards the door. "Get lots done today before the men take time off!"

"Yes, ma'am," he bowed regally before heading out the door.

Piper was still smiling as she washed up the last dish before placing it in the rack. She dried her hands and pictured what her mother's joyful expression would be like as she stepped out from her car and took her first good look around her daughter's ranch. Piper decided, *she'll love it here almost as much as I do.* She just knew her parents were going to be very proud of her. When Sawyer came back inside a few hours later to help her prepare lunch, she'd already laid it out on the table. Ham and cheese omelets, home fries, and toast.

"Get the guys in here," she prodded, "before everything gets cold."

Her enthusiasm for dinner was equally robust. Thick sirloin steaks with baked potatoes made on the barbeque. Later that night, relaxing with Sawyer on the sofa in the living room, she told him she'd never been happier. Had never felt so satisfied with her own efforts, her home, and her life. Before he even responded, she could see in his eyes that he felt the same too.

"While the men are off for a few days, we'll do a little bit of celebrating on our own," he smiled.

She panicked for a second, thinking he had something romantic and sexual planned. Although she loved him, she wasn't quite ready for that yet.

"Yup, I'll take you to Gatsby's Fine Grill for dinner over in Carling. You'll love the place. They have the best continental cuisine for miles around."

"Oh, that sounds fantastic," she sighed, relieved that he only had a romantic dinner in mind. "Isn't Carling the town about thirty miles from here? I've heard of it but haven't been there yet."

"Well, that'll change tomorrow. It's as fancy a place as they have around here, so make sure to put on your best dress."

"Noted," she laughed, wondering if her slightly low-cut black velvet dress would be a little too much.

She spent most of the next afternoon getting ready for their date. *Date,* she actually said out loud when Sawyer wasn't in the house. They'd never truly had one of those. Which really was kind of crazy since they'd grown so close and already professed their love. She was humming to herself cheerfully, looking for something to wear, when her cell phone rang on top of her dresser across the room. She picked it up and gasped. James Garrett. Her first thought was that there was something wrong.

"Mr. Garrett?" she sounded hesitant.

"Yes, hello, Piper. How are you today?"

His tone was carefree and jubilant, so there was obviously nothing wrong.

"I'm actually doing great, thanks for asking. Is there something new going on with my divorce?"

"Yes, but before you panic, it's all good news this time."

"Thank God," she blurted, laughing. "Give it to me all at once then."

"You asked for it," he chuckled. "Have you heard of a company called Megaforce Associates?"

"No, should I have?"

"Probably not. It's a holding company of a numbered corporation that's owned by your soon-to-be-finalized ex. That huge debt that John says he owes? Well, my forensic accountant has done some digging, and it turns out that John owes the money to himself."

"What does that mean?" Piper asked, still too hesitant to think the absolute best.

"It means, my dear, that John's debt prohibiting further payout of funds for your divorce settlement is invalid. The money is all there, and it's his. I've already emailed Matthew Stephens informing him of his client's faux pas. And, of course, I insisted that you receive all funds owing immediately, including retroactive payments."

"Mr. Garrett, you're a genius!" Piper screamed.

"Not really, but don't ever tell my wife that," he laughed.

When Sawyer came to the house later to pick Piper up for dinner, he was astounded to see how beautiful she looked. He'd never seen her dressed to the nines before.

"Too low cut?" she asked him.

"Are you kidding? It's perfect. You're perfect and stunningly gorgeous tonight."

"Thanks," she said as she took his arm. "And by the way, dinner is on me tonight."

Fifty-Three

"CLOSE YOUR EYES," Sawyer instructed before leading Piper into the main barn. "OK, open them and have a look around."

"Wow!" she gasped, barely believing what she saw.

Everything was finished, brand new, and shiny where it wasn't wooden. Even the barn beams looked spotless in the sunlight gleaming through the windows.

"It's so airy and clean," she remarked.

"Don't get too used to clean," he chuckled. "That'll soon change, as soon as we start bringing in cows."

"Oh, right," she smirked. "I guess I'll have to get used to the sweet scent of cow manure."

"Let's just say there's nothing else like it," he laughed.

"So, everything's done then?"

"Just here, in the main barn. We still have a lot left to go in the rest of the barn and still tons of work to do outside."

"But this...this is fantastic!" she smiled, moving forward and taking him in her arms.

The men had finished for the day and left to go wash up for dinner, so she and Sawyer admired the renovations all on their own.

"Oh, I was going to tell you later, after supper. I checked my account, and all of the money John owes me has now been deposited into my account. When you get a chance, add up what I owe you, and I'll pay you back."

"OK," he smiled. "No rush. I trust you."

After she took a closer look at the completed work, they wandered to one of the nearest pastures on the east side of the barn. It was huge and flanked by woods in the distance, a forest that was also part of her ranch.

"I've been thinking," she mused, as they headed slowly towards the trees, "why don't you make a riding trail in there so, when we get horses, we can ride through the woods."

"You've ridden before?" Sawyer looked at her skeptically.

He'd thought Piper was a city girl through and through.

"Well, no," she admitted, "but you can teach me. How hard can it be to sit on a horse, after all?"

If she was at all irritated by his laughter, she didn't show it. He quickly explained that horseback riding was a skill fraught with danger, and she'd be likely to acquire more than her fair share of bumps and bruises as she learned. He explained that even the best-trained horses aren't always obedient, so she knew exactly what she was getting into. Instead of changing her mind, Piper insisted he build a couple of stalls as soon as possible in the so-far-unrenovated back end of the barn. They would buy two horses, one for each of them.

"I'm thinking Percherons, like in my painting," she exclaimed with a smile.

"Luckily, that's a great choice," he told her. "They're pretty docile, great for beginners. I don't see you breaking too many bones starting out with those."

"Very funny!" she punched him playfully on the shoulder. "Seriously though, when do you think you'll get their stalls done? And how long do you think it'll take us to find two Percherons that are already well-trained?"

He could see by the sparkle and determination in her eyes that she'd found her new passion. Luckily, it was one that he could share with her.

"With the guys' help, maybe a week or two. We might as well build a few horse stalls while we're at it because I see you in the future wanting to expand the herd."

"Great!" she hugged him. "I'll start browsing and looking at horses for sale tonight!"

The next morning, Tim and Jeff were surprised when Sawyer pulled them away from their projects to help him renovate the horse section of the barn. When he explained it was for Piper and how excited she was at the prospect of buying horses and learning to ride, they understood.

"Nothing like a good woman's wish to keep you working hard and on your toes," Jeff laughed. "We've been there, buddy. We'll help you get everything all set for the horses as quick as we can."

So, Sawyer mused, the guys aren't surprised by my relationship with Piper. He asked them how long they'd all known.

"Oh, I'd say from the development stage," Tim smirked. "Seriously though, I think we could see it coming long before you did. We're actually surprised it took this long!"

"Yeah, well, I guess I'm a slow mover," Sawyer joked. "Until now, that is. She's already starting to look for horses, so unless I want to be in the doghouse, we'd better get this finished in the next few days."

By the time Sawyer brought Piper into the barn four days later, she'd already found a couple of Percherons for sale only about fifty miles away. Two young mares. One, a beautiful speckled white, and the other, a lightly speckled gray. Both with gorgeous white flowing manes. They went to see them together the very next day. The seller agreed to truck them. By the time they arrived a few days later, Piper had already hand-crafted and painted their wooden nameplates to place on the outside of the doors to their stalls.

"Whisper and Willow," Piper gushed proudly as Sawyer screwed the plates into the wood. "I'm so glad I love their names and won't have to change them."

She was beside herself with excitement when they arrived. She spent so much time during the day watching them graze in their pasture and so much time standing outside their stalls and talking to them at night that Sawyer was left with most of the cooking for the men those first few days. Eager to get on Whisper or Willow's back, she plagued Sawyer with constant questions about how soon he could help her learn to ride.

"First, you get used to grooming and handling your horse on the ground," he told her the next Saturday as they brushed the horses outside. "The important thing for you to always remember is that the horse you handle and control on the ground is the *same* horse you ride."

"In other words," she caught on quickly, "if I can't keep her safely under control when I'm doing groundwork, I can't expect her to behave any differently when I get on her back."

"Exactly," he nodded. "Build up your confidence with the horses while you're on the ground. Win their trust and respect before you think of mounting."

They took Piper's lessons slowly, but Sawyer was leading each horse around the pasture with Piper sitting on its back by the end of the following week. It took her quite some time to master walk, trot, and canter, but eventually, she did and was so proud of herself. In the meantime, some of the men were clearing a long riding trail in the forest. It ended in a large natural meadow halfway from the furthest property line.

The cattle were ready by the time Piper and Sawyer rode into the forest for her first ride. They attended the auctions together. Although he knew what he was doing, Sawyer constantly asked for Piper's input and explained what he suggested. This had begun as *her* dream, and he didn't want to take that away from her. When he explained the rationale for artificial insemination instead of getting a bull, she still insisted on buying a live animal. He relented, making her promise she'd never minimize or ignore the dangers and would stay clear of it and always on the other side of the fence.

Their foundation herd was small, but Sawyer had never seen Piper so happy. As the end of summer neared, her parents came for a visit, and he delighted in helping her give them a tour of the ranch. For a while, he couldn't think of anything else he could do to make their lives even happier. Until he saw an online ad for beagle puppies for sale close by. He remembered her painting of the beagle by the fireplace and how she'd said she really wanted to get a dog just like that one day. He surprised her with a little eight-week-old male that she named Champ.

For the longest time, Piper thought her life couldn't be more perfect. Until Sawyer surprised her again.

Fifty-Four

"IT'S LIKE HEAVEN OUT HERE," she said as she spread their tablecloth down on the grass in the meadow.

They'd ridden there, tied the horses, and were having a picnic at the meadow's edge, in the shade under a tall oak tree.

Putting the fried chicken and potato salad onto their paper plates, she asked him for the slices of bread as he handed her their cans of iced tea.

"Damn, I left the bread on the kitchen counter!" he winced. "Want me to quickly go back and grab it?"

"No," she laughed. "I'm starving, and I don't want to wait."

"Luckily," he smirked, his eyes twinkling, "I *didn't* forget everything."

She gazed at him curiously as he searched through the picnic basket he'd packed, and she was stunned when his hand emerged holding a small black jewelry case. Before she could ask him what he was doing, he opened it to display a gorgeous, shiny diamond ring. Positioning himself properly onto one knee, he took her hand.

"Piper, you already know how much I love you, and I'm hoping you love me as much too. Will you do me the honor of marrying me?"

In shock, she lowered her plate onto the tablecloth. The world was spinning, and she was sure she'd never known such joy.

"Yes!" she exclaimed in excitement.

"Yes?" he looked relieved.

"You bet!" she smiled and dove into his arms.

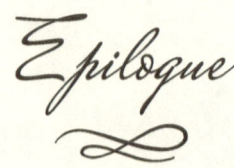

Epilogue

"DON'T FORGET to take videos too," Sawyer told Tim, handing him his phone as he walked past on his way to the barn.

By the time Sawyer reappeared, leading their new white pony into the sand ring, Piper had already come out of the house. It was a beautiful, warm summer day filled with sunshine. The type of weather when memories are made. Smiling, Piper walked up to the pony and laughed.

"No way, Sawyer! A pink saddle?! Where did you ever find that?"

"Had it made special," he chuckled, "just for today."

Tim aimed Sawyer's phone camera and moved closer as Piper placed the giggling toddler in her arms onto the saddle. The little girl squealed in delight.

"You like her, Ainsley? Her name's Princess, and she's your very own pony!"

Ainsley wriggled and kicked her chubby legs.

"I think she's saying let's get moving," Piper laughed, looking at Sawyer. "Ainsley, tell daddy, let's go."

"I think she's going to grow up to be just as impatient as her mom," Sawyer joked as he slowly began leading Princess around the ring.

Walking along and holding her little girl firmly as she giggled in the saddle, Piper couldn't believe that time had gone so fast. It seemed like her doctor confirmed that she was indeed pregnant just yesterday. On this day, three years ago, her miracle baby was born. Sawyer had promised to get her a pony the very first time he held her in the hospital room. If Piper hadn't made him control himself, he probably would have purchased one that same day. There's loads of time, she'd told him. She convinced him to wait until their daughter was old enough to understand that one of them was truly all hers.

"Before you know it," Sawyer looked back at Piper and their daughter, "she'll be riding the trails in the woods with us."

"Oh, I'd give that at least another year," Piper joked.

Sawyer led Princess around the ring several times before Ainsley got restless. A true horsewoman to the core. When finally, she seemed to be getting a little tired, Piper plucked her off the saddle and took her back to the house to give her lunch.

"I lost count of how many videos I took," Tim said. "I probably got at least a hundred or so pics to add to the thousands already on your phone. At this rate, bud, you might have to increase the memory on your phone," he laughed.

Later that afternoon, after Piper laid Ainsley down for a nap, she and Sawyer sat relaxing together on the back porch.

Stroking Champ's head when he curled up beside her on the bench for a snuggle, Piper asked Sawyer, "Do you think we're spoiling Ainsley too much?"

"Is there such a thing?" he laughed. "Nah, I think it's pretty normal we want to give her the world."

"Yeah, but at some point, I think we'd better tell her that the whole world isn't hers," Piper laughed.

"Some point, maybe. Not today."

When Ainsley was born, they'd vowed to give her the very best life possible, and they already weren't too far off from that. In just a few years, their hard work had paid off. Their herd of cattle had grown by leaps and bounds. They'd purchased over three hundred head of cattle, and eight new calves had been born at their ranch just today. Since Piper had taken up showing horses, their horse herd had expanded. Their prize show horse was now worth well over forty thousand, with someone already offering half that for her unborn foal. Despite their amazing success, they'd remained humble, never forgetting for a moment to be grateful and how hard they'd worked to build their life together to get this far.

"Sawyer?" Piper asked, as she laid her head on his shoulder, "Do you ever wonder what our lives would have been like if I'd caved in years ago and sold the ranch?"

"No," he hugged her tightly to him as he answered. "I'm convinced that never would have happened. We were destined to be together from the start. I've never met any woman as courageous and smart or as resilient and beautiful as you."

"Well, thank you," she smiled as she sat up to look at him before leaning forward to kiss him. "I love you with all my heart too."

THE END
Did you enjoy *Counting on the Cowboy*?
Please consider rating it on Bookbub or Goodreads, or your favorite retailers.

Have you read ***Focusing on the Cowboy***?

Join my Newsletter for new releases, sales and other promotions at www.daisylandishromance.com